ONE SITKA SUMMER

ONE SITKA SUMMER

FAITH AND FRIENDSHIP ON THE ALASKAN FRONTIER, 1867

LOIS LINDENFELD

ONE SITKA SUMMER
FAITH AND FRIENDSHIP ON THE ALASKAN FRONTIER, 1867

iUniverse books may be ordered through booksellers or by contacting:

iUniverse
1663 Liberty Drive
Bloomington, IN 47403
www.iuniverse.com
1-800-Authors (1-800-288-4677)

ISBN: 978-1-4917-4885-5 (sc)
ISBN: 978-1-4917-4884-8 (e)

Library of Congress Control Number: 2014917446

Printed in the United States of America.

iUniverse rev. date: 02/06/2015

CHAPTER 1

―――∿∿∾∘᠑⟨⟩᠐∘∾∿∿―――

"Watch yer step, missy," said one of the sailors on the *Alexander II* out of San Francisco. "I don't wanna trip you up now."

Eliza Healy carefully stepped over the coils of rope that lay on the deck. "Good afternoon, Rome," she said to the crusty old sailor as she went to the rail at the waist of the ship.

The stiff breeze sweeping in from the Bering Sea whipped about her, causing Eliza's homespun linsey-woolsey dress to billow out. She shivered as the cold air hit her legs. Her black stockings did little to keep out the wind. She pulled her thick blue shawl tightly around her shoulders with one hand. With her other hand, she pushed her black bonnet farther down over her ears and held on to it as the brim flapped in the wind. Flung loose by the wind, strands of her blonde hair tangled about her freckled face.

Eliza watched the craggy cliffs as the schooner glided by. The peaks were covered with snow, and countless waterfalls cascaded down the slopes to the icy water below. Farther along, where the trees grew near the shore, large birds with white heads soared above the sea, making a clucking trill as they flew. She had heard the same sound before and knew that they were eagles, but there were so many eagles here!

Eliza marveled at the wildness of the Alaskan shoreline. Her family had left San Francisco six weeks earlier, and Eliza was ready to get on solid ground again. *I hope we get to Sitka today,* she thought.

Father had told her that Sitka was the Russian governing center for the Alaska Territory. The Russians had called it New Archangel, but it was known by its Tlingit name now, Sitka.

Eliza was startled when she heard the sailors bellowing commands to prepare for arrival. During the voyage, these sailors had made the time pass more quickly for the passengers by singing bawdy songs and telling stories of whale and seal hunts with the native Alaskans who lived along the sea. Now the sailors seemed to sing out the commands as they brought in the giant sails and tied them to the masts. The sails flapped and snapped loudly in the strong wind, almost drowning out the sailors' shouts. Other seamen were readying the four small skiffs to put into the sea.

Eliza strained to see where her family would be living. They would gather the equipment and supplies through the Russian-American Company to set up a mission church among the natives. Their small church in Wisconsin had raised money for them to come and build the new church.

As the ship rounded the next point and neared shore, Eliza's excitement plummeted. She saw two ragged rows of white tents facing the sea, stained with mud two feet up each side. Men in dark, ragged clothes strode through the makeshift street. Others appeared to be wearing large furry coats with hoods. Eliza could make out shaggy dogs romping and barking or sleeping among the tents.

Eliza looked up the main street of Sitka, lined on each side with two-story wooden buildings, weathered gray. A wooden plank sidewalk ran along one side of the muddy street. Three cross streets from the waterfront, Eliza glimpsed a large gray-white building. Two tall, onion-shaped domes towered above the roof. Each dome had an unusual cross with three crossbeams, not just one. The two near the top were different lengths, and a slanted one crossed midway down the shaft of the pale. Just then, the bells in the domes rang out across the grimy town to the sea.

"Are you ready to start your new life in Alaska?" Eliza's father asked as he came to stand beside her.

Eliza glanced over her shoulder at her mother, who stayed near the captain's cabin to shield Eliza's little one-year-old brother, Amos, from the wind. Mrs. Healy tightened her heavy woolen shawl around both herself and Amos. Her mother was using all her strength to keep from being blown over. Amos had multiple layers of clothes on, but he still snuggled into his mother's shoulder to keep warm.

Eliza turned to her father. "Father, there's a church here already. Why did we need to come? Why does it have those domes?"

"You are full of questions today," Father laughed. "That's the Russian Orthodox church. The domes identify it as a church, just as the steeple, bell, and cross identify our church back in Wisconsin. It was established by the Russian government. It's the only church allowed in Russia for almost a thousand years. When they brought the Finnish carpenters to Sitka, Russia allowed them to establish a Lutheran church here too. It is in the small building across the street from the Orthodox church."

"Why did we need to come to plant a church if there are churches here already?" Eliza asked.

Eliza's father continued, "As you know, we belong to the Evangelical Brethren Church. We teach that salvation is a gift to us from God. Our faith is in God alone, not our works."

"Then why are we working to bring our church to Alaska?"

"The works we do are given to us by God and because we love God. It is our desire to do His work to build the church here on earth," her father answered.

Eliza knew this, but she didn't know God's work would be in such a place. She had been excited as her family planned to come to Alaska. She had heard reports about the beauty of the Alaskan seacoast. Stories about the natives and their culture had sounded so exciting. She was curious and thought it would be such a great adventure, but Sitka was not what she had imagined. Since Sitka was the capital of Alaska, she had imagined a big, bustling city, not this run-down, rugged, forlorn town. She felt fear rising through her stomach to lodge as a lump in her throat. She realized that *loving* God and *serving* God were very different.

A huge splash interrupted Eliza's thoughts. The sailors had just dropped the anchor. Eliza quickly grabbed the railing; when the anchor caught on the bottom of the harbor in Seattle and Vancouver, Eliza had flown across the deck.

"I see you have learned to grab the railing so you don't fall." Father's eyes sparkled, reflecting the setting sun.

The ship's anchor dragged across the bottom of the sea. The ship glided and then lurched to a stop when it came to the end of the anchor chain.

Pointing toward a small hill, Father continued, "If you look over there, you will see Baranof Castle on Castle Hill. That is where the Russian governor lives and works."

Castle Hill rose above the sea on the right side of Sitka Bay. At the top perched a large white wooden building. The building was surrounded by a stone wall and appeared to be a fortress. At the bottom of the hill, small buildings dotted the waterfront.

"Is the governor a king? The castle looks more like a big house than a palace," Eliza said.

"Governor Baranof was appointed by Peter the Great, the tsar of Russia. He is in charge of the Alaska Territory and determines what happens here. He is not a king, though," Father said. "There is also a fine school. Father Iakov has been teaching the Alaskan young men to be priests so that they can go back to their villages to start Russian Orthodox churches. He is teaching them to speak English now. It became official this month that the United States owns Alaska. William Seward tried for a long time to purchase it. This October, Alaska will be turned over to the Americans, so the natives will need to know English."

"Is there a school for girls?" Eliza asked.

"Yes," her father said. "There is a small school where the Russian and Tlingit girls go so they can learn English too. They also learn to read, write, and do ciphers."

Eliza was surprised to see that Sitka was also surrounded on three sides by a tall wooden barricade with evenly spaced guard towers. A shipyard with a half-finished ship sat at the far side of Castle Hill. To the right, she could see buildings with large waterwheels run by the water that poured down the hill. The lumber was next to one, and a few grain sacks were stacked next to the other building. The first building was a sawmill with giant saws powered by the waterwheel, and the other was a grist mill that ground wheat and corn into flour.

"Father, why are there two large square riggers at the wharf? How will we get to shore?" Eliza asked.

"Those are Russian ships. It is about fifty yards to shore. Our American ships cannot dock yet; unfortunately, that means you can take a skiff, or you can swim," Father replied, grinning.

"Why can't American ships dock?" Eliza asked.

"These are still Russian waters until the territory is transferred to America in October," Father said. "Our ships need to ask permission to dock. Our ships can only dock if there are no Russian ships and if we have permission."

At that point, several passengers jumped over the rail into the frigid water, howling and gasping for air when they came up. Other men on the ship either threw their trunks into the water or lowered them on a rope. Each man took a piece of baggage and began swimming toward shore. Eliza watched wide-eyed as several women tucked the backs of their homespun skirts into their front waistbands and jumped overboard too. They began swimming toward shore, pushing carpetbags ahead of them.

Eliza placed her hands on each side of her face and gasped and stared at her father. "I can't jump into that water. It's freezing cold! Look! There is ice still floating in it!" Since Eliza was already chilled to the bone, her teeth started chattering as if she were a stuttering monkey.

Father smiled. "No, I arranged for your mother, you, and Amos to ride in one of the skiffs. If everyone waited for a skiff, we would still be traipsing cargo to shore until tomorrow. Since the ship is leaving at first light, we need to get our things off tonight. They need to load it up again for the trip south to San Francisco. So I'll be swimming. I want to claim the tent I reserved for us and prepare for when you come ashore." And with that, Father put his hands on the rail of the ship and flung himself over the side, clothes and all.

A sailor tossed one of their trunks into the water. Father came up with his amber eyes as large as apricots. He gasped for air, let out a howl, and grabbed the trunk. At first, he pushed it as he swam. When his feet touched bottom, he hefted the trunk to his shoulder and started for shore.

"Come on, missy," Rome said, pointing to a small boat. "We need ta git you inta a skiff and gitcha to shore. I gotta heapa trips to make taday. Go git yer ma, and bring some of the wooden boxes ta put inta the skiff."

Although the skiff was small, Eliza thought it would be a lot warmer and drier than wading to shore. Eliza helped her mother drag four of the smaller cases to port side. Eliza also kept an eye on Amos, who loved to hide among the barrels on deck. It had been his favorite game on the long voyage. His chubby cheeks and easy smile made him a favorite among the crew and other passengers.

Rome loaded the smaller cases of dishes into the skiff and then lowered it into the water.

"Wait! You forgot us!" cried Eliza.

The sailor laughed. "You'll need ta skedaddle down the rope ladder. You kin do it faster than old 'nezer over there."

Eliza glanced at the old storytelling sailor who sat on the deck, mending a sail. She ran to him and threw her arms around him. "Good-bye. You take care of yourself."

"You take care of yourself, missy," Ebenezer said as he readjusted his pipe. "There's plenty bears in them there forests, not to mention those wild men."

Eliza smiled and waved and wondered what he meant.

CHAPTER 2

E liza returned to the rail and peered over. A rope ladder swung
wildly against the side of the ship. From the deck, it was a
fifteen-foot drop to the skiff. How would she and her mother with
baby Amos ever get into the boat?

Rome opened the small gate in the railing. "You first, missy," he
said. "Then I'll come 'alfway down the ladder. Your mother'll hand
the baby ta me, and I'll hand him ta ya. When you git the 'ittle one,
sit in the bow of the boat. Then I'll he'p the missus down."

Eliza turned and let herself slowly down until she felt a rung
beneath her black, high-top shoe. As she put her weight on the first
rung, the smooth sole of her shoe slipped to the side of the rung,
almost causing her to lose her balance.

"*Ow!*" cried Eliza as the rough hemp rope tore bits of skin from
her palms. It was much harder than going down a regular ladder like
the one she had climbed down from her sleeping loft back home in
Wisconsin. It stayed still and was smooth from wear. Regaining her
balance, Eliza slowly descended the pitching ladder.

As she got near the boat, she was swinging back and forth and
up and down as the ship rolled from side to side with the waves and
bobbed with the wind. "Oof, oof, oof," Eliza moaned as her body
slammed against the side of the ship. Surely, the gray-green sea was
reaching up to grab her. She felt as if she had never done anything
so difficult. As the ship rolled, she was nearly dipped into the water.
When the ship rolled to the other side with the waves, she felt the

ladder pulling her up until she was almost lying flat on the side of the ship. Finally, she stepped into the rolling skiff and looked up to see how far she had come. The side of the ship seemed as tall as a house. It creaked and shuddered as it rolled back and forth in the water.

Eliza watched the sailor climb halfway down the ladder. He asked Mother to hand down the baby. It looked too far for Mother to reach. She knelt down by the opening in the rail, hugged Amos, and gently held him over the side. Holding on to the rope ladder with one hand, the sailor grabbed one of Amos's legs with the other.

"I got 'im," the sailor said. Mother let go of Amos. Eliza held her breath. Mother screamed, thinking that Amos was falling into the sea. The sailor hung on to Amos's foot and swung him smoothly around in a large, smooth arc.

Everything seemed to be happening in slow motion. Amos's arms and legs spread straight out stiffly. His fine blond hair looked like a halo about his head. Eliza wasn't sure whether Amos was laughing or screaming as the sailor brought him down until he dangled by his foot above Eliza's head.

Eliza stretched on tiptoe, rocking the boat, but she couldn't reach him. The green slime and rough barnacles on the lower side of the ship smeared her dress and cut into her arms. She tried again. Suddenly, the ship rolled toward her, the ladder dipped into the skiff, and Amos came to within her reach. Amos had an ecstatic smile on his face. His red face and laughter made her laugh too. After Eliza had Amos safely in her arms, he held his arms toward the sailor and squealed, "Do gan?"

"Easiest way ta do it, ma'am," the sailor said with a grin. "Done it many times. They luvz it."

With Amos squirming in her arms, Eliza scrambled to the front seat. The sailor climbed the rest of the way down the swinging ladder.

"Okay, missus, I'll he'p you inta the boat," Rome said.

Eliza knew that her mother was frightened by the wild-eyed look on her face as she looked at the ladder swinging back and forth against the side of the ship. Eliza's mother brushed nervously at a loose strand of hair with the familiar look of determination Eliza had come to know. Mother put her foot on the ladder, which was still pitching against the side of the ship. The sailor held it firmly from below, which steadied it some. Rung by rung, Mother came slowly down to the boat. The last rung was wet, and her foot slipped.

Eliza gasped and held Amos a bit tighter as her mother fell into the sailor's arms. The boat tipped, causing the load in the skiff to shift and topple. The sailor stayed steady since he was used to keeping his balance on a rocking ship or boat.

"Oh dear. I am so sorry," Mother said, smoothing down her skirt and adjusting her hat.

"Happ'ns all da time," Rome said with a toothless grin.

Mother primly took her place in the back of the skiff. She looked off to the mountains as she quietly composed herself. Eliza almost laughed at her mother's discomfort. Instead, she gave Amos a kiss on his head.

The sailor began rowing to shore. The dark, threatening clouds that had been drifting in from the sea let loose a deluge, soaking everything. The little boat rocked as the cold waves washed over the bow of the boat and engulfed Eliza's feet. As her eyes scanned the twinkling lights of the fires and lanterns on the shore, Eliza thought of the warmth of her grandmother's house and of her family and friends back in Wisconsin. Her tears joined the constant shower of rain and the spray of cold seawater. She was glad no one could see them. Eliza realized that life in this cold, windblown town would not be so easy. She wasn't sure she was equal to the task God had given to her and her family.

CHAPTER 3

When Eliza got to shore, she dragged the boxes from the skiff and slumped down on the family's trunks. A roaring fire had been built to warm those bringing in the luggage. The raindrops spit and sizzled on the huge red-orange logs. The intense fire helped to dry the belongings. Eliza held Amos on her lap as the other passengers ran back and forth on the beach. Both she and Amos were shivering and soaking wet. Mother retrieved a quilt from one of their trunks and wrapped Eliza and Amos against the cold wind, and Amos soon fell asleep in Eliza's arms. Eliza closed her eyes.

Their mother gently nudged them awake. They had dried off by the roaring fire, which was now burning to hot, golden-orange embers. Father and the other men had set up tents for all of the families. Their trunks and boxes were already inside of their gray-white tent. The other passengers gathered their things, which dotted the beach like black spots on a Dalmatian.

Mother took Amos and placed him on her hip. "We need to collect some driftwood from the beach so that I can cook some corn mush for supper," she said. "I'll take Amos, and you can find some rocks for a fire ring and dry wood for our fire."

Eliza easily gathered enough stones from the beach to make a fire ring. Most of the driftwood was still wet. The sea-bleached driftwood that lay farther back from the sea was drier and would burn. Thinking ahead, Eliza tugged wet driftwood farther up the beach near their tent so that it could dry for future use.

By the time she returned to the tent, her mother had pulled their thin straw mattresses from a trunk and made their beds on the floor. The tent was an eight-foot by twelve-foot rectangle. It wasn't even as large as Grandmother's kitchen back home! Eliza wondered how long her family would need to live in a tent. Mother had already hung their pots and pans from the ridge pole that reached across the peak of the tent's roof. Her trunk with her few things sat next to her bed. Mother and Father's bed was against the other side. All of their other belongings were stacked along the front and sides of the tent.

When the corn mush was done, Father came to their tent. "I'll build up the fire, and we can gather around it to keep warm and eat," he said as he threw more wood on the fire. He rubbed his hands together over the flames. "Everyone's trunks are in their tents in a jumble, but they are in."

After supper, Father built up the fire for the night just outside the flaps of the tent. Eliza found her flannel nightgown, quickly put it on, and fell into her bed. Father put the lantern out and plunged the tent into darkness. Eliza thought the patter of rain on the tent roof and the roar of the waves made lonely sounds in the night. She felt a fine mist as the rain seeped through the separations in the woven material. This was not like her home in Wisconsin. She would be dry and snug in a warm bed. The sturdy logs of her house made her feel secure, not at the mercy of whatever might claw through a canvas tent. She was used to the owls calling and the other night noises of Wisconsin. This was not the adventure she had thought it would be.

In the night, Eliza suddenly woke up and heard men shouting and singing. "Buffalo gals, won't ya come out tonight and dance by the light of the mooooon?"

Where am I? Then she realized that she was rolled up on a mattress inside a tent. It was very cold as she stepped from under her quilt. She could see her breath in the light that flashed through the tent flap. She grabbed her shawl and went to see what was going on.

11

As she made her way to the flap, a large man suddenly stumbled in. The acrid smell of his sweaty clothes and the alcohol on his breath made Eliza shrink back to her bed in fear.

He staggered about and shouted, "Why the heck are you in my tent and in my bed?" Then his eyes focused on Eliza, and he slurred, "Oh, sweetie, maybe I can just get in bed with you, and you can keep me warm."

Eliza screamed. The tent was filled with shouting, pans rattling, confusion, motion, and Amos's cry as Father leaped up from his bed and clutched the burly man's arm. "Let me take you home, sir," he said sternly as he guided the man from the tent.

The drunken man's yelling and cursing faded away as Father directed him down the row of tents. Dogs began to bark and howl. Other voices were shouting out in the black night. Eliza's mother was trying to calm Amos's cries. Eliza huddled under her quilt. Her heart still raced, threatening to burst through her ribs. Rain, wetness, darkness, and fear all crowded in around her. *I can't do this, God. Why did You bring my family here?*

Father came back to the tent. She peered at him as he stood silhouetted in the opening, backlit by the dying embers of the fire. He threw on a bit more wood and then came to her bed.

"Are you all right?" he asked.

"Yes," Eliza quietly lied.

Amos had fallen asleep again. The dark shadow of her father crawled into bed next to the sleeping ball that was her brother. He reached his arm across to touch her mother on the shoulder. Her parents quietly talked about the drunken man. Then she heard them praying for their mission work and safety among these rough men as she fell into a fitful sleep.

Eliza woke cold and wet from rainwater that had soaked through the canvas roof of their tent. Her toes felt numb. She pulled her feet up inside her nightgown and tightened her grandmother's quilt around her body. Her grandmother had made the quilt for Eliza before she left Wisconsin. As she buried her nose in the quilt, Eliza could smell Grandmother's scent of fresh-baked bread and rosewater that still lingered faintly in the fabric.

"Eliza, it's time to get up," Mother called in from the fire pit. "I need you to watch Amos while I cook breakfast."

With a groan, Eliza turned over and surveyed her new home. Amos sat in the middle of the rug spread on the floor, playing with the wooden horse their father had carved for his first birthday. Mother had thoughtfully laid out her everyday clothes, a sweater, and her blue fringed shawl next to her on her trunk.

When Eliza moved, Amos squealed in delight. His warm baby breath hung in a frosty cloud above his head. He toddled to where she lay wrapped in her quilt. He could barely move, because he had on several layers of clothes. She laughed as he jumped on her, shouting, "Iza! Iza!"

"Just you wait a minute, Amos," Eliza said softly. "I need to get dressed. Can you find my shoes?"

As Amos tottered to the tent flap where her shoes were drying, Eliza quickly pulled her stockings on to warm her feet. She reached out, pulling the dress off her trunk and into her bed to warm it up. She slipped her nightgown off, staying under the covers. Sitting up under her quilt, she slipped on her chemise, hooking the hooks that ran down the front. By squirming and lifting her body, she was able to pull on her petticoat. After stopping to catch her breath, Eliza struggled to get her gray linsey-woolsey dress over her head, buttoning up the front. By then, Amos was back with her shoes. She grabbed the sweater from her trunk and ventured out from under the quilt.

"Brr," she mumbled as she scrunched up her freckled face. She quickly put on her shoes, thankful that her mother had warmed them by the fire. She thought her toes might actually thaw out. She drew on her heavy woolen sweater and wrapped herself in her shawl. The cold still penetrated through her petticoat and homespun skirt. Eliza ran her hand over her fine blonde hair. It stuck out in all directions and was twisted and tangled from her struggles to get dressed. It needed to be brushed and braided.

"Mother, where is the hairbrush?" asked Eliza.

"It should be on my bed," her mother called back.

Eliza found it behind the mattress of her parents' bed. She pulled it through her pale golden hair. "Oh no. The brush is all wet," Eliza called out.

"Amos was playing with it. He probably had it in his mouth," Mother replied as she cooked and stirred the porridge.

"Eew. I'll have spit all over my hair," Eliza scolded. "Amos, don't suck on the hairbrush!" As she glanced down at him, he stood with his arms up so that she would pick him up.

"That little grin will get you nowhere with me," she teased as she hugged him. "Do you want to brush my hair?"

Amos took the brush and banged it into Eliza's hair and pulled down. "Ouch!" she cried. "That will be enough of that." She made a few more passes through her hair and then braided and coiled it around her head, pinning the hair in place with the hairpins from her trunk tray. Amos squealed as he tried to brush his own short hair. When she was finished, she took Amos by the hand and headed outside.

"Breakfast is ready," Mother called.

"At least the sun is shining today. Maybe it won't be so cold," Father said as he sat down on a log by the fire. "I hope I can get some more food supplies. I talked to some men down the way, and they said food is in short supply. I like mush and porridge, but the corn and oat flour we brought from San Francisco is getting low. Something else to eat for a while would be nice. I'll start asking around for lodging too."

As Eliza stirred her porridge, she hoped he'd find other things to eat too. They didn't have butter, milk, or sugar for the oat porridge. She had eaten it for six weeks on the ship. She was ready for her mother's savory venison stew and fresh bread. With the supplies that came on their ship, at least they would have wheat flour to make bread.

"What do you mean the food supply is short?" asked Mother.

"Russia doesn't bother to send ships anymore. It is too far and too expensive. There is a law that says foreign ships are not to sail into Russian waters. That will change as the day of the transfer of Alaska nears and it becomes an American territory. I'd thought the colony was self-sufficient by now. Hopefully, once Alaska becomes an American territory, we will be able to get food from California. The companies there are more than glad to bring food and trade for the furs trapped here," Father said.

"The *Alexander II* brought sacks of grain," Eliza said. "It brought chickens and a few cows to trade for furs. We should be able to get eggs and milk."

"Yes, and I hope to get some from the people who bought them, but I will probably be on a waiting list to get anything," Father said, shrugging his shoulders. "I will try to get on the list today."

Eliza scanned the beach and the muddy tents she had seen from the ship. Scruffy men sat by a small fire, holding cups of hot coffee. There were tents farther down the shore with families wearing beaded and embroidered hooded fur coats. The other tents nearest theirs temporarily sheltered the men and women who had arrived with them on the ship.

"Who are all those men and families down there?" Eliza asked. "They must have lived in those tents a long time."

"The families in the parkas are Aleuts," said Father. "The Russians brought them here from the western islands to hunt sea otters and fish and to trap furs for the Russians. The others are looking for gold in this area. The tents to the south are the gold miners'. After the gold rush in California in 1849, men started moving on up the coast in hopes of finding more gold. They have just begun arriving in this area."

Eliza thought it would be exciting to go looking for gold too until she remembered the man from last night. A shiver ran down her spine.

"Let's get our Bibles and have our devotions while we keep warm by the fire," suggested Father.

Eliza fetched their Bibles while Mother filled their mugs with hot coffee. Eliza brought her parents' Bible and the new one she had received for her last birthday. She also brought the cloth book she had made for Amos with pictures of stories from the Bible. It had helped her learn many of her stitches that all accomplished young girls needed to learn. It was much more fun than making a sampler of the alphabet and numbers as her cousins had.

Father began, "I am reading from Galatians 5:13. 'You, my brothers, were called to be free. But do not use your freedom to indulge the sinful nature; rather, serve one another in love.'" After a sip of coffee, Father continued. "That is why we came to Alaska, to serve others through love. We need to remember that God expects us to love all people just as He does. So we need to love the gold miners next door, the Russian people who live in Sitka, and the Tlingit, Aleuts, and other natives who live in this area. God has given us the freedom to love, but we must not use God's freedom in ways that are selfish or unkind."

"What are the freedoms that come from our sin nature?" asked Eliza as she puzzled over the scripture.

"We have the freedom to do both good and evil. But we should always choose the good. Last night, a miner stumbled into our tent because he was drunk. I had the freedom to become angry at him and just throw him out, or I could serve him with love by taking him to the right tent. If I followed what my sin nature told me to do, I might have been pretty rough on him, but love told me to handle it in a kinder way. He wasn't used to all of the new tents on the beach, and he was confused. His tent used to be fifth from the first tent, but with the new tents put up last evening, his tent is the tenth one," Father explained. "Now let us pray for a good day in our new home and that we can serve all of the people in this area."

After devotions, Eliza asked, "Can I walk down the beach and back?"

"Don't go far. Always keep the tent in sight," her father said as he headed to the general store.

"No, I need your help here," said Mother as she began picking up dishes to put in the pot of hot water on the fire so they could be washed.

"Can I help you later?" Eliza asked. "I just want to look around a little."

"Then take Amos with you," Mother replied without looking at Eliza. She brushed a wisp of hair from her face with the back of her hand. "After these dishes, I need to organize our things a bit better. We quickly dragged them into the tent last night, and I cannot find a thing. Then I hope your father can find supplies so I can bake some bread. So don't take too long."

"Do I have to take Amos? He will slow me down," Eliza said.

"It's the least you can do since you aren't going to be here to help with the things that need to get done." Her mother sighed.

"Come on, Amos. Let's go for a walk," Eliza said, resentfully taking him by the hand.

CHAPTER 4

Eliza shaded her eyes and glanced up and down the beach. The tents were on a flat area about forty feet above the high-tide line. To the west, Eliza could see the verdant green islands with frosted mountains across the narrow inland channel. They had traveled the inland channel all the way from Vancouver, so Eliza was familiar with the islands along the way. As she looked south, she saw the craggy mountains they had passed the day before. In fact, Sitka was surrounded by mountains covered with snowcaps.

To the east, three mountains of equal size were completely covered in snow. She had read in a book that they were called the Three Sisters. The contrast of white snow, deep evergreen forests, sky-blue water, and sunlit sky made her feel as if she were standing in a painting.

After a moment to marvel again at God's creation, she decided to walk north toward the town instead of down the beach past the miners' or Aleuts' tents.

As they walked, Eliza noticed a young girl coming down Castle Hill. *She looks as if she might be about my age,* Eliza thought. The girl shaded her eyes and seemed to look toward Eliza. She was carrying a large basket filled with colorful cloth. When she reached the bottom of the hill, she went up a side street that led to a snowcapped mountain.

Eliza and Amos continued up the beach, pausing to pick up rocks and shells.

"Look at this pretty shell, Amos," Eliza prompted. "Feel how rough it is."

Amos turned the shell over in his hand. He picked up another shell to show Eliza. "Look, Iza!"

Eliza picked up a rock and threw it into the water. It made a loud plunking sound. Amos danced in delight. He began picking up rocks and trying to throw them into the water, causing Eliza to laugh too, since they flew in all directions.

The sun felt warm on her face even though clouds and wind were coming in from the sea. It was the first time that Eliza had been to a beach since she had come across the Atlantic from Sweden when she was five.

"*Pree-vyet,*" said a quiet voice.

Eliza glanced up with a start. In front of her was a girl dressed in furs. She was slim and tall. Her dark brown, curly hair framed her face as if it was an extension of the fur of her hood. Eliza admired the fur parka with the fur-edged hood. Strips of red, black, and white ribbon in an intricate design decorated the front on each side of the placket where the parka was closed. *Maybe this was the girl from the fort. Was she speaking Russian?*

The girl tried again. "Hell-oo."

"Oh, hello," Eliza said. "Do you speak Russian?"

Very slowly, the girl replied, "*Da,* I know little English. I learn in girls' school."

"I know English and Swedish, but I don't know any Russian," Eliza answered as she picked Amos up. "What is your name?"

"My name Katrina Voronov. I live near barracks. Mother wash clothes for governor and priests. I bring down to her. My father guard fort."

"Very nice to meet you. My name is Eliza Healy. This is my brother, Amos. He is a year old. I am fourteen. My father came here to build a church. My mother takes care of us and helps Father."

"Your brother sweet. I am fifteen. My brother is Maxim. He sixteen. He give me headaches." Katrina went on with a grin, "We have church in Sitka. It big. Why your father think he build other church?"

"Alaska will soon become part of the United States of America. We have many kinds of churches. My father wants to build a church that worships God as we worship in America," Eliza said. "The Russians let the Finns build a Lutheran church, and we will build a Brethren church. The Brethren Church is the third-largest church in Sweden."

Wrinkling her brow and looking unsure about what Eliza had said, Katrina said, "*Da*, I know the States people come in October. The Russian people go back to Russia. I do not know what my family do. My father and brother like to trap furs. There many furs here."

Clouds began to cover the sky, and the wind picked up from across the water. Eliza wrapped her shawl around Amos. "I really like your coat and hat. It must keep you warm."

"Yes. You get a warm coat?" asked Katrina.

"I have seen coats like that when frontier men from northern Wisconsin visited our town, but I don't know if I can get a warmer coat now. We don't have much money, and most of it is for building the church. Our friends from our church back home gave us money so that we could serve the people here. They collected and saved money for a long time to send us. I don't think my father would spend it on anything else."

Katrina looked puzzled. "I saw you ... from Castle Hill. Not many girls here. I want to meet you. I hope we be friends, but I hear Meti calling me."

"I would like to be friends. I left my cousins and friends back in Wisconsin. But now I need to get Amos back. He has fallen asleep. When will I see you again?" Eliza asked.

"Meti and I finish wash. We have more to do each day. We meet here sometime?" Katrina asked Eliza.

"Let's meet soon. I'll be watching for you. My tent is the fifth one," Eliza said, holding up five fingers and pointing to her tent.

"*Da-svee-da-nee-ye,*" Katrina said as she turned to go. "Oh, good-bye."

Eliza watched Katrina walk back toward town. Katrina stopped and waved before she passed the corner near the Russian Orthodox church.

Eliza chattered as she took Amos back to the tent. "I can learn some Russian and help with her English. *Pree-vyet, da-svee-da-nee-ye.* Well, my pronunciation isn't very good. I can't wait to see her again. We'll become good friends."

Suddenly, darker clouds swept in, and it began to rain. But for the first time, Eliza was excited and happy about being in Alaska. She had already made a friend. But just as soon as her day had turned happy, she was cold, wet, and alone again. Carrying a sleeping Amos, she ran to her tent.

"What took you so long?" her mother asked sternly when she arrived at the tent.

Eliza glared at her mother's back as she bent over the fire. "I can't even have ten minutes with a new friend," Eliza mumbled under her breath as she laid Amos on the bed. Her mother was so busy that she didn't even hear her.

CHAPTER 5

Katrina ran up the mud street past the Russian Orthodox church and turned down the street toward Castle Hill. She could hear Meti still calling for her. She turned up Barracks Street by the Russian army barracks. As she passed Princess Maria's grave, she paused, curtsied, and crossed herself, and then dashed on. As she rounded the corner to her house, she almost collided with her mother.

"Where have you been?" she asked Katrina in Russian.

"After I delivered the laundry to the castle, I saw a girl my age that got off the ship yesterday," Katrina said. "I only went to say hello to her. I only stayed a moment."

"Well, we have more laundry to do, and I need your help," Meti said. "We need to get the robes done for the priests and the altar cloths for the church. Now hurry."

On the back porch, Meti had set up three tubs. She had already filled two of them with boiling hot water, and steam roiled from the tubs in the cool spring air. Meti had rolled up the sleeves on her black dress and wore a woolen scarf tied in back over her hair. Her black apron was still crisp and clean, but that would change as they did the day's work.

Katrina hung her parka on a peg, rolled up her sleeves, and tied a scarf over her hair too. Then she brought the baskets of priestly robes to her mother. They would need to be done first to honor the priests.

Her mother had been scraping bear tallow and lye soap into the first tub with a knife. She took one robe at a time. With a long wooden stick, she stirred the robe about in the tub until it was thoroughly wet. She plunged the stick up and down, agitating the soap and water through the cloth. Using the other end of the stick, she scooped up the cloth from the tub and allowed the water to drip back into the tub and let the cloth cool a bit.

Then Katrina took the robe and began to wring it with her bare hands. She needed to squeeze as much water from the cloth as possible, trying not to lose any of the hot water from the first tub. When she was satisfied, she put the robe into the second tub of hot water. She also had a long wooden stick and stirred the robe about in the tub to remove as much soap as possible. Then she lifted it from the tub and wrung it again. Finally, she placed it in the tub of cool water and stirred again to remove the last of the soap. Again she lifted the robe from the tub and wrung it out. Placing it in a basket, she took it to the clothesline strung across the back of the porch, where she hung it up to dry. On sunny days, they would hang the clothes in the fenced backyard.

When Katrina got back to the washtubs, her mother was already at the second tub, wringing out the second robe. Katrina took the next robe and put it into the soapy water in the first tub. By alternating tasks, their hands didn't get so tired from wringing out each piece of clothing.

As Katrina and her mother worked side by side, she began to tell Meti about Eliza. "Meti, she is my age and has blonde hair and freckles. She is very pretty."

"What is her name? Why did they come from America?" Meti wanted to know.

"Her name is Eliza. Her parents came to build a new church," Katrina told her.

"But why would they want to build a church? We have two already," Meti asked. "Our cathedral is beautiful. The Finnish shipbuilders have a Lutheran church across the street from the cathedral."

"There will be more Americans coming next year, and they are going to build a different church for them. I guess they have many churches in America," Katrina said, puzzling over the reason to need different kinds of churches.

"The Americans will do as they wish when they are in charge. There is just one God, and so we have one church. Russia has survived for many years with one church," Meti said as she came to take her turn at the washtub.

"I think the Americans can use our help," said Katrina. "Eliza just has a sweater and a shawl to keep her warm."

"Ah, this we can do," said Meti. "One thing our church teaches is to take care of each other, to help others. This will help us do good and please God. Then He will look on us with favor."

"But what can we do?" Katrina asked.

"Let me think for a minute."

Katrina looked about the back porch. She noticed her brand-new parka that Meti had just made for her. "I know! What are we going to do with my old parka?"

"It is too small for you. We will probably be going back to Russia. Your father hasn't decided yet, but if we do, we will need to get rid of many of the things we have collected over the years. So we will probably need to leave it behind."

"Meti, could I please give it to Eliza? She is a bit shorter and smaller than I am," said Katrina. "I'm sure it will fit her."

"*Da*, that is a good idea," said Meti. "We can do a good deed, and then God will bless us."

The water in the first tub was gray from washing the robes. They couldn't put the nuns' white habits or altar cloths into such dirty water. "We can take a break while we heat up some water for the rest of the laundry," Meti said. "How about some bread and tea?"

"My hands could use a break, and I need to warm them up," Katrina said. "I will build up the fire in the yard and fill the cast-iron cauldron with water. It can heat up and be ready when we are done eating."

As Meti was filling the samovar to make the tea, the front door burst open, and a rush of cold air almost put out the fire in the front room fireplace. A tall young man entered and dumped a pile of dead animals on the living room floor.

"Maxim, get those dead animals out of my house. You know you need to put them in the backyard!" Meti shouted.

"Aww, Meti, I have just come down off the snowy mountain, and I'm freezing," Maxim complained. "Let me have a cup of that hot tea to warm me up."

"*Niet*! Not until you get those animals out of the house!"

"Look. I got a silver fox," Maxim said as he held up the dead animal.

"Out!" Meti said as she pointed to the back door.

Reluctantly, Maxim picked up the dead animals and went to the back door. Just as he opened the back door, Katrina was trying to come in. Suddenly, there was a loud scream, and Maxim laughed loudly.

CHAPTER 6

It was another dark, gloomy day, and a cold, light mist hung in the air. It had rained daily for the last week. Father had not been able to find much food at the store. He was able to get a small amount of flour from the grist mill and a couple of eggs from the German woman who ran an eatery on the main street.

"The people of Sitka are slowly starving. Since the Russian Fort Ross closed in California, no supplies have been shipped to Sitka for months," Father told them. "The Russian men are afraid to go into the forest to hunt or out to sea to fish, because they fear the Tlingit who live in the area. They attacked the fort a few years back. No one leaves the Russian fort without soldiers to protect them in the event of an attack. It is difficult to find game in the forest with so many men tramping along. Supplies brought on the American ships go quickly. It will be a waiting game for the next ship."

After lunch, Eliza peered through the tent door. As she dried and put away the lunch dishes, she scanned the beach for Katrina like she had each day.

Suddenly, she saw a small figure coming down the beach, but it didn't look like Katrina. Something big, round, and dark was moving down the beach. Suddenly, it cut across the beach and headed for Eliza's tent.

"*Pree-vyet*," the figure said.

"Katrina, is that you under there? What are you carrying? Come in out of the drizzle," Eliza jabbered.

"Dreezzle? What is that?" asked Katrina as she put her bundle on Eliza's trunk.

"It is a soft rain," Eliza's mother said. "Hello, I'm Eliza's mother, Mrs. Healy."

"*Och-en pree-yat-na*," said Katrina, giving a small curtsy. "I am please to meet you."

"What did you bring?" asked Eliza.

"I bring you fur parka. My parka new. Meti make it from Father's furs. Old parka ... too little for me, but fit you. If we go back Russia, we need give way. I do not have little sister or brother to use for," Katrina said as she unfolded the bundle. "It for you."

"Oh, Katrina, I can't take your parka," Eliza said as she held the lovely parka up to her. "It must be very valuable." It was made of dark brown strips of fur. An attached hood was trimmed with a longer fur of blended gray and cream.

"Meti said I give to you. It just bear fur with wolf fur 'round hood," Katrina said. "These furs hard to trade. Russia not pay much. They want sea otter, marten, mink, or wolverine fur. We give you this parka in the name of God. The priest say we must do these good things."

"It is a special blessing to us," Eliza's mother said.

"Can I try it on, Mother?"

"Yes, a parka will keep you warm," Mother commented. "Thank you. It is so very generous of you and your mother, Katrina."

The parka fit perfectly. Eliza hugged it around her. "I don't want to take it off. Thank you so much, Katrina."

"You do not need to take off," Katrina said with a twinkle in her eye. "The Tlingit sleep in coats in winter. They teach how to be warm when we come. You need fur blankets for winter."

"It has been cold at night. How cold is it?" asked Eliza.

"It freeze in April night. Warm when sun shine," Katrina told them. "It be warm soon. Time to celebrate when sun shines."

Mother sat on her bed, her dainty hands folded in her lap. "How long have you lived here?" she asked.

Katrina counted out five fingers. "I … five when my family left Okhotsk, Siberia. Father sent here … work for governor who sees over Russian America. I live here ten years. My mother, father, and brother come here. I never used to cold wind that blow in from the sea. I glad my friend, Erm, taught Meti how make fur parka. She not make fur coat before. Woman make for us in Siberia," Katrina told them.

Motioning for Katrina to sit on her bed, Eliza sat cross-legged on the carpet. "Does it rain every day?" Eliza asked.

"Rain, snow almost every day," Katrina said. "My father say it rain or snow forty-two *archin* last year."

"*Archin?* How much is that?" Eliza asked.

"Sorry, that 'bout one hundred inches," Katrina laughed. "We learn 'bout inches in school."

"That is a lot of water!" Eliza exclaimed. "I will be fifteen in November," she continued. "Erm? I have never heard that name. Is that a Russian name?"

"No, she Tlingit. Her family at fishing camp in mountains now. They fish for eulachon (hula- gon) to make oil, hunt … trap animals. Their home south of Sitka, next to river. She come to girls' school … learn English last summer. I cannot wait 'til she come back. She very fun; I think you like her. We all be friends," Katrina said.

"Father said the Russians are afraid of the Tlingit. They fear attacks. How can you be friends with Erm if she is a Tlingit?" asked Eliza.

"The past be bad. Village and tribes to north not like Russia to be here. We careful of tribes in north. Erm's village small. They learn it be good to be friends," said Katrina. "Her tribe have trouble with tribes of north sometimes. They like war."

If Erm was from a friendly tribe, Eliza couldn't wait to meet her. "I want to learn about the Tlingit. Are most of the people around here Tlingit?"

"These men here, not Tlingit," Katrina went on. "Men in tents are rough and loud. They from all over world. The Norwegians,

Finnish, Chinese come for trade or business. The Americans come now. They come to find gold. At night, they and the *promishylniki* go to saloon, get drunk, shout, and sing loud."

"Who are they?" asked Eliza.

"The *promishylniki* are bad men from Russia. They make come to work for Russian company. They do hard ... labor. You need be careful of the *promishylniki*."

"Are they robbers or murderers?" Eliza asked, wide-eyed.

"*Da,* very bad. Live in huts near Russian barracks. The other tents are miners' tents. Clothes always muddy from rain and digging for gold. Sometimes they come to store to get things. If Meti and I are in store, they say bad ... words about Russians. They do not know I learn English for two years, so I know they say bad things."

"We heard them the night we arrived. They woke us up in the middle of the night. Are they dangerous?" Eliza asked.

"The *promishylniki* are. They fight and steal," Katrina warned them. "But the miners, not so bad."

"We will be alert to the *promishylniki*," Eliza's mother said.

"Who are the people wearing parkas?" Eliza wanted to know.

"They are Aleut. The Russians bring ... from islands near Siberia ... to trap seals, fur, and fish," Katrina said. "Russian soldiers not know how. The miners go look for gold in day. They come to town at night. When they not drink, they can be very nice. Most men married. Have children in America. They want gold ... bring families to Alaska. Some women here now."

"Do the women stay in the tents or go out to help the men with the gold?" Mother asked. "I would like to make friends with them. Maybe all of the women will want to study the Bible."

"Bible? What is that?" asked Katrina.

"God inspired men to write the Bible so we can know God," Mother said as she picked up her Bible. "It has many stories and lessons that Jesus taught."

Without looking directly at the Bible, Katrina said, "We cannot read the *Bee-blee-ya*. Only priests at church can read it. They say we be … blind if we look on words of God. They have … pictures on walls of church. People can know what God say from pictures. Do you read this Bible? I would not want to be blind."

Eliza stared at Katrina for a moment in disbelief. *Why would they say it would make her blind?* Eliza took her Bible and turned to Psalm 119:103–105. She began to read, "'How sweet are Your words to my taste, Sweeter than honey to my mouth! Through Your precepts I get understanding; therefore, I hate every false way. Your word is a lamp to my feet and a light unto my path.'" She explained, "God's word is sweet like honey. Reading the Bible must be a good thing. God wants us to live in the right way. We can do right by studying the Bible ourselves. Then we know what God wants us to do. God's word shows us our way. I read the Bible every day, and I'm not blind."

"I see," Katrina said with a frown as she looked at Eliza's eyes closely. "Someday, I take you Saint Michael's Cathedral. Father Iakov can tell you about church. You see the beautiful icons that tell us about God."

Eliza rose from the carpet to her knees, leaning forward eagerly. "That would be interesting! I would love to see the pictures and meet Father Iakov. Maybe I can come to school with you this summer. Could I, Mother?" Eliza said.

"I will talk to your father about that," Mother replied.

"Is Father Iakov a strict teacher?" asked Eliza.

"No! You cannot go to Bishop House School. Father Iakov not teach at girls' school. The Bishop House School only for Tlingit boys. They be priests. Tell villages about the Russian God. Girls must go to girls' school," Katrina said. "It start to rain hard. I go home before I swim home. I come when Erm be here."

After Katrina left, Eliza considered all that Katrina had told them. If Katrina liked Erm so much, she thought she would like her too. But how different would she be? Would Erm's tribe shoot arrows at her like the Indians did on the plains? After all, she was an American, not even a Russian.

CHAPTER 7

—⟍⟋∿∘ᕤᘓᕤᘓ᙭ᘐᘓᕤ∘∿⟍⟋—

I n the mountains north of Sitka, Saankalaxt Erm's dark eyes gazed down the river toward the coast. Erm's family was getting ready to move to their permanent village near the Indian River. It was the fourth moon, and the snows were melting. Soon the sun would melt a little of the snow each day. At night, it would freeze again into ice. There was always the chance that there would be an avalanche as the snow melted on the peaks above.

The fur of Erm's parka framed her round face and collected the lightly falling snow. It might rain near the sea, but it still snowed on the mountain. The fishing had been good that year, and her family still had dried bear and deer meat left. When they were at the village, they would be eating the sweet salmon caught from the Indian River that flowed to the sea. They would dry what they didn't eat for the next winter.

Erm trudged back to her temporary home at fish camp, which was built of cedar bark over poles made from small trees. The floor was just dirt, and already it was turning muddy from the melting snow. Her father, her mother, and her brother and his wife and baby daughter lived with her in the one-room house.

Erm's family belonged to the Eagle Clan, the Burnt House Tribe, and the Wolf House. People died and people were born, and they came and left. But Erm belonged to the clan, and the clan would always be there as it had for generations past.

Saqua nudged her leg. All of the dogs were barking excitedly. Father had just come from the *gowa* with another load of belongings to put in the large canoe. The canoe was made from one large cedar trunk. Her father and uncles burned out the center of the log. Then they chiseled out the burned wood and had made the sides as smooth a sea otter fur. It was fifty feet long and would hold her whole extended family. On the bow, a beautiful eagle was painted on each side. There was room for eight rowers in each canoe of the Burnt House Tribe.

When Erm's family got all of their things into bundles and bentwood boxes, her mother and sister-in-law would take down the Cedar bark of the *gowa* and place them in seal bladder sacks to protect them from the weather.

"Hurry, Erm. We must get going before the moon falls into the sea," her father said.

"Yes, Father, I will go get my bundle," she said. Each person would place his or her bundle in the canoe. Erm had packed her extra tunic, leggings, baskets, and bags made from seal bladders she had made, along with whalebone needles, leather and gut strips, small beads made from shells, a cooking pot, a bowl, and a beautiful carved sheep horn spoon. She placed everything in the middle of her bearskin blanket and folded it all into a neat, tightly wrapped bundle. She tied the bundle securely with twine made from the fine roots of a cedar tree.

When all was ready, the family stood in the center of the floor of what had been their *gowa*. Father stretched his hands to the sky. "Oh, Raven," he called, "you have caused the earth to provide for us. We ask you to go with us to the sea. As the earth peeks from the snow and the rocks are black from the cold, we leave this place. Watch over it, and replenish the land and rivers with animals and fish before we return."

Just as he finished, a raven flew overhead, calling out its loud, cawing cry. The raven had heard Father, and Erm's heart lifted in awe.

All of the family groups in Erm's tribe had their own canoes, although Erm's Wolf House family had the largest one. Everyone picked up the bundles and loaded them into the canoes. Her father and uncles wouldn't row the canoe. Prisoners the clan had captured from other clans or disgraced members of their tribe would row. The members of Erm's family were considered wealthy, and people of their caste did not do the hard work of the tribe.

After her family was in the canoe, the rowers pushed the canoe into the water and then jumped in. As they began rowing, the canoe glided quietly through the waters of the river to the sea. The family members laughed and joked with one another. It would take them over two days to get to their permanent home on the outskirts of Sitka.

When the sun began to ride the horizon, Erm's father told everyone to be quiet. Erm turned and saw three deer, a buck, a doe, and a fawn, on the shore of one of the islands that protected the inland passage. Islands buffered this channel from the cold. Erm's father raised the Russian rifle he had traded furs for and took aim. With one shot, he took down the large buck. The doe and her fawn leaped and dashed into the forest.

The canoes landed on the sandy beach. As the men skinned and cut up the deer, the women built a fire and got pots from the canoes. The deer was just enough to feed the entire tribe. Each member had the same amount, regardless of his or her position in the tribe. They would camp there for the night.

Erm was excited about going to their permanent home. She would go to the girls' school in Sitka. She learned a little of the strange language the last two summers. The native children from the tribe only attended school for four months during the summer.

* * * *

In their tent by the sea, Eliza and her mother were knitting heavy gray sweaters as Amos napped on his parents' bed. Eliza was making a sweater for Amos while Mother made one for Father. They would make sweaters for themselves later. It was a good thing that Father had been able to buy the yarn. There were few supplies at the general store. Father had still not been able to buy much food. They would need to wait until the next American ship came. No one knew when that would be. Father was able to purchase some wood at the sawmill, but there were no nails available. He bought a length of wire from which he would cut and sharpen nails. He would need to make dovetailed frames that interlaced at the corners. Her family had only come with their bare necessities, so her father would need to buy materials to make their furniture and for her mother to make clothes for the family.

Her father was outside in the rain, making bed frames for the mattresses. Getting the mattresses off the floor would keep them drier and warmer. In the summer, Eliza and her mother would stuff the mattresses with fresh grass or pine needles.

Suddenly, Eliza heard someone shouting excitedly, "Eliza! Eliza, come quick!"

Father smiled and said, "Your friend Katrina is running down the beach."

"May I go see what she wants?" Eliza asked her mother.

"Of course," her mother answered.

Eliza rushed out of the tent. "What is it?" she asked.

"Our scouts to north say Tlingit come back," Katrina said. "Erm's family come from their fishing camp. They be here soon. Maybe Erm ask us come to village. You meet Erm and her Tlingit family. Their village very different from anything you see," Katrina said excitedly.

Just then, the nose of a large cedar canoe appeared at the end of the outcropping where the Aleut tents sat. It was filled with many people in parkas with the hoods pushed back. Many dogs barked, and children waved to the people who had collected on the beach. More canoes of various sizes soon quietly glided beyond the outcrop of rock and filled the Bay of Sitka. Each canoe was filled with adults, children, dogs, furs, and containers of all kinds, piled high.

Eliza could see the large Tlingit paintings on the bows and the sterns of the cedar dugout canoes. Bright red, yellow, black, and white were used to paint each of the animal figures.

"What do those pictures represent?" Eliza asked Katrina.

"The eagle on front tell us they are Eagle Clan. On back, picture for houses are painted. See there, a frog, a turtle. Look for wolf; that be Erm's family," Katrina told her.

There was a tall Tlingit warrior standing in the back of each canoe, wearing a bright red blanket with various black-and-white figures woven into the fabric. Each man stood proud and with his arms folded across his chest. Each man wore a cone-shaped hat similar to a Chinese man's hat. It was woven in light-colored reeds with dark designs woven from cedar root strings to make lines and figures in the hat. Attached to the top of the hat was a small woven cylinder with a small figure attached on the top. Eliza could not make out the figures on the hats. The last canoe was the largest of all. A wolf was painted on the sides at the back of it, and eight men rowed it.

"Oh, oh! There! There Erm!" shouted Katrina as she jumped up and down, pointing at the large canoe.

In response, a young girl held up her hand in a salute.

"See her?" Katrina yelled, waving her hands at Erm.

Eliza was spellbound. She had never seen such a glorious sight. She waved her hand tentatively as the canoes glided on through the bay, staring at the sight of the ten canoes crowded with bundles, dogs, and people. The last of the canoes soon disappeared beyond view as they headed to the opening of the Indian River.

"The tribe was up north to cold river that bring eulachon fish from icy lakes in mountains. They use oil from eulachon to do many, many things," Katrina told her.

"What things?" Eliza asked.

"I not know all. Make medicine, keep food, cook, keep bugs off, and more things too," Katrina answered. "Erm will let me know when they be ready. Then we go to her village."

Eliza could not imagine what Erm's village would be like. It seemed that it would be large when she saw all of the people who were in the canoes. "Is her village big?" she asked.

"No, not big. Raven Clan north of town very big," Katrina said. "They live by fort wall. Father took me to stand on stockade; you not see end of their village. They not as friendly as Eagle Clan where Erm live. We afraid of Raven Clan."

Concerned, Eliza asked, "But Erm's village is friendly?"

"Yes. They not make Russians mad," Katrina told Eliza. "They afraid Russians attack them. They be friendly. We help them; they help us."

"When do you think we can go?" asked Eliza.

"I will let you know, but I go home. Meti need me come home to finish wash today," Katrina said as she turned to go, giving Eliza a wave. "Good-bye."

Eliza waved back and watched Katrina run back up the beach.

Suddenly, Mother screamed. When Eliza turned around, she saw Amos toddling toward the beach. A huge wave was rolling toward him. Eliza knew that when such a wave ebbed to sea again, it would be too strong for Amos to get back to shore. It would pull him under. Amos was squealing in delight as he ran on tiptoes toward the waves. Eliza raced for the shore. She knew she must reach the shore before the wave crashed, dragging Amos under.

Eliza watched the wave as the water pushed it taller and faster into shore. Stumbling and nearly falling, she raced as fast as she could, counting the seconds and watching the speed of the wave. By now Mother, Father, and others were all headed toward the beach. Would someone get to Amos in time?

Eliza grabbed for his arm, but Amos's feet were being washed from under him, and he fell face-first into the icy water. Eliza stood in horror as she watched Amos disappear beneath the pounding waves.

Katrina came back when she heard all the shouting and stood by Eliza as they watched the shadowy figure of Amos under the water floating farther and farther from shore.

Suddenly, there was a large man dashing past Eliza and running into the water. He fought against the huge, cold waves. When he got to Amos's body, he reached out his hand. The big burly miner from the first night pulled Amos out from under the water by the seat of his pants. The man laid a limp Amos on the beach and pressed up and down on his chest several times. After many attempts, Amos coughed and sputtered as seawater spilled from his mouth and nose. Then he bawled. His cry rattled in his lungs. Mother came with a blanket, wrapped Amos in it, and hugged him to her. Tears ran down her face. Amos was shivering and had a pale blue tint to his skin.

Eliza could not move. The icy-cold waves rolled over her feet. It swirled around the hem of her dress and petticoats. Everything had happened so fast, and yet it had seemed to be in slow motion. The loud shouts of the people had sounded like low, tortured moans. Then Amos's cry pierced the air. Eliza slowly turned and saw everyone on the beach crowded around her tent. She stood alone in the water, feeling her feet go numb. She hadn't been able to do a thing to save her own baby brother. Now he was very ill.

"I'll go to get the doctor!" someone yelled as he dashed off. A flash of red hair disappeared behind the row of tents.

"Come, Eliza," said Katrina as she took Eliza by the arm.

Eliza slowly walked up to her tent. The crowd parted so that she could enter. Her mother sat on her bed, crying and rocking Amos, bundled in blankets. Her father, leaning over Amos, was praying with his hand on the bundle that was Amos. Amos, crying and coughing, spit up water from time to time. Eliza knew the salt water would burn if it got into a broken wound. What would it feel like in a baby's lungs?

Dr. Strobel arrived at the tent. He listened to Amos's chest and took his temperature. "He has a slight fever, and there is a great deal of fluid in his lungs. The body can only stand a small amount of extra salt. Since the salt is in the lungs, it's going directly into his bloodstream. We will need to watch for pneumonia. Let me know immediately if his temperature goes up or if he has trouble breathing or is spitting up blood. In the meantime, get as much water and liquids down him as you can. It will help wash the salt out of his blood. If he doesn't improve, we may need to bleed him, but he is so small. Here is a tonic to put into his water. It will reduce the fever and is also a painkiller. Only put two drops per bottle."

After the doctor left the tent, Eliza asked in a quiet, choked voice, "Is there anything I can do to help?"

Father looked from Amos to Eliza. It almost seemed like he forgot she was even there. Finally, he said in a flat, lifeless voice, "Yes. Empty the medicine bottle that has the least medicine in it. Wash it thoroughly with freshly boiled water. Then fill it with more boiled water. Let it cool."

As Eliza went to the trunk where they kept the medicine chest, her father quietly called to her, "Find the rubber nipple we brought. It should be in that trunk too."

Eliza saw that the castor oil bottle was about empty. She was glad to pour that out. As the bottle soaked in hot soapy water, she rummaged through the trunk, looking for the nipple they had brought in case Mother couldn't nurse Amos on the trip from Wisconsin to San Francisco. They hadn't needed to use it. It seemed to take a long time to complete what her father asked. Finally, she brought the clean, cooled bottle to Father.

He held the bottle up to the light and carefully put two drops of the tonic into the bottle. He placed the nipple on the bottle and handed it to Mother.

Mother's eyes searched Father's face as she took the bottle. Eliza could hear her father quietly praying as Mother but the bottle to Amos's dry, cracked lips. A drop of the liquid landed on his lips. Amos turned his head and began to cough again. Patiently, Mother continued to try to get the medicine down. Finally, he tried to suck the liquid into his mouth. As he tried to swallow, he gagged and then coughed again.

Eliza sat on her bed watching the scene. Each time Amos cried or coughed, her tears began anew. "Oh, God, dear Jesus, forgive me for not watching Amos more closely. I know Mother always wants me to help keep an eye on him, but I didn't. Now he might die. I am so easily distracted from my responsibilities. Forgive me for my weakness. Please, please make Amos well again. Why did You allow this to happen to such a small child? It doesn't seem fair. I would rather take his illness to pay for my sins. It is only right that I should be the one to suffer, not Amos. Oh, help us, Jesus."

Chapter 8

Erm swung the basket of fish heads to her shoulder. She lugged the basket from where the women of the village cleaned and filleted the salmon to dry on poles set on wooden tripods. Erm had been busy all morning carrying raw fish heads to the sandy area near the bay. She had already dug a hole in the sand and gathered seaweed from the beach to prepare the Tlingit's favorite delicacy.

She followed the forested path and quietly sang songs to the fish heads, asking them to forgive the people for taking their lives and thanking them for giving their lives so that her people could live. There had been fewer and fewer salmon these days as the first salmon canneries opened at the mouth of the rivers. She sang the song so more salmon would return to her tribe's river.

Suddenly, a dark shadow fell across her path. Erm looked up and saw Monutat, a tall, lean hunter of the Raven Clan. He was bare to the waist with deerskin pants and mukluks. A beaded belt hung over his left shoulder. His cropped hair was decorated with a cone-shaped hat with a carved, painted raven on its flattened peak. He had reached the age of twenty summers and was at the Tlingit age to marry. She quickly averted her eyes. She was not allowed to look at a man directly in the face.

Monutat greeted Erm with a typical Tlingit greeting. *"Yak si zee xwsateni,* Erm? Where are you going?"

He was taller than most of the men, and Erm thought he was very handsome. He was considered a hero in the area because of the animal meat he brought to families who were running low on food during the winter. He had often stopped by to visit with her father and check on her family. Erm knew that he watched her go about her work as he talked with her father.

Now Erm inclined her head, always keeping her eyes down.

"May I help you carry the basket to the river?" he asked as he lifted the basket from her shoulder.

His hand touched her arm, and a shiver coursed through her body as he went ahead of her. Erm glanced at Monutat's back in surprise. What was this strange feeling?

When they got to the river, Monutat dumped half of the fish heads into the seaweed-lined hole that Erm had dug. Erm went to get more seaweed from the pile she had gathered and placed it in the hole over the fish. She spread the seaweed so it completely covered the layer of fish heads. Then Monutat dumped the other half of the fish heads into the hole, and Erm placed another layer of seaweed. This was the third basket she had brought this morning. The fish heads were within six inches of the top of the hole. She filled the hole with more seaweed and then salty seawater. Erm covered the hole with a large piece of cedar bark. Monutat brought a large rock from the riverbed to weigh down the bark. Erm glanced at Monutat as he placed the rock on the cedar bark. His muscles flexed under the weight.

They did not speak to each other but worked side by side, making the Tlingit's favorite food—raw, fermented fish for the winter.

After Monutat finished placing the rock on the cedar slab, he turned and began digging another hole in the sand.

"No, I will do it," said Erm. After all, making fermented fish heads was a woman's responsibility.

Monutat sat on a large rock. She could feel his eyes on her, and she felt warm at the thought.

When she was done, she laid the shovel on the ground and walked toward the path that led to the village. Monutat picked up the basket and joined her.

"You are a good worker," Monutat said softly. "I think you are a strong woman. *Tula-aan.* Responsible."

Erm knew Monutat meant more than his words communicated. It meant that he liked and admired her. It was a talk of love. Erm took a quick glance at Monutat's face. This action was a signal to Monutat that she accepted his compliments. Erm also saw the smile that filled his face as her eyes lingered. Again, she cast her eyes down.

What could this mean? She was thirteen summers old and not yet a woman. She had not been through the woman's ceremony. Since a member of the Eagle Clan only married someone from another clan, she could be married to a warrior from the Raven Clan. Was it possible that Monutat planned to have his uncle ask her aunt whether he could marry her?

* * * *

Every night, the tide was low, and the crashing of waves seemed far from the tent. Early in the morning before the tide came in, people could dig for crabs and catch small fish and other seafood that came into shore. In May, the tides were even lower as the weather became warmer.

Father woke Eliza early one morning, because he had heard the tide would be especially low. It was a good time to collect mussels from the rocks that normally were underwater.

Rubbing her eyes, Eliza dressed and stumbled from the tent. The beach was alive with people collecting mussels and other sea creatures stranded among the rocks and in the tide pools. Eliza took a bucket and moved farther along the beach where there were fewer people milling around. Ravens, gulls, and eagles soared and cawed out. They dove for the fish and sea creatures that lay exposed on the shore. To avoid a collision with the ravens, Eliza put her arm over her head and kept low to the ground. The ravens were bold and noisy, scolding her for her intrusion.

The beach was a whole different world that had been hidden deeper in the water and invisible to Eliza. Large rocks jutted from the exposed sea bottom. Each rock was encrusted with black mussels. Wedging a knife blade under each mussel, Eliza popped them off into her bucket. As she looked for the larger ones, she discovered starfish stranded above the tide line. Some were thick and crusty, while others had long, skinny arms that looked like little snakes coming out of a bright orange shell. Spiny sea urchins sat like flowers among the rocks. Seaweed lay thickly. Little fish darted about in the pools of water left behind by the tides.

Eliza saw movement out of the corner of her eye. About thirty yards out, playful harbor seals bobbed their heads above the surface of the sea. Baby seals darted and leaped out of the water, chasing each other. They all darted underwater, soon popping up again. Eliza giggled as she watched them. It reminded her of the playful antics of puppies and kittens.

Several Tlingit canoes floated several yards offshore. Two men were in each canoe. With intense interest, Eliza watched the men cast nets over the side of the canoes. A silvery, flipping mass of tiny fish came up in the nets. Father had told her that it was time for the run of herring that came as the waters warmed. They came in huge schools that filled the waters of the bay. It seemed to Eliza that new and exciting things happened each day in Alaska. There was so much to take in and learn.

Not far behind the canoes, small puffs of steam seemed to rise from the waves. Then Eliza heard the loud trumpeting of a whale. At that moment, the monstrous nose of a black-and-white snout rose from the sea several feet into the air. Its back arched and twisted as it plunged beneath the water. Its huge tail flipped into the air and then slapped the water as the whale plunged beneath the waves again. The spray showered over the men in the nearest canoe, and all of the canoes were rocked by the waves. Eliza gasped as she raised her hand to her mouth. She couldn't believe how large the whale was and how close it had come to the small boats.

The men were shouting and singing. They stood in their canoes, reaching into the sky with harpoons. They drew in their nets and paddled quickly to the mouth of the Indian River. Eliza wondered why they didn't stay to harpoon the whale.

Eliza wandered farther down the beach while she watched for more whales. Suddenly, she heard voices singing and chanting. Not twenty-five feet in front of her, a large, flat rock jutted out into the sea. Five Tlingit women stood on the rock, and they all had their hands raised. One woman chanted as she looked to the sky. Others danced in small, delicate steps.

Eliza hid behind some bushes to watch. When the chanting was over, the women leaned over at the edge of the rock. They began pulling cedar limbs from the water. Clinging to each branch and needle hung strings of tiny white sacs. The women stripped them off and placed them in baskets. When each branch was cleaned, they placed the branches back into the water and tied what looked like heavy brown string to them and to large stones on the large rock on which they stood. They lifted their baskets to their shoulders or hips and disappeared into the forest.

Even farther down the beach, a short Tlingit girl was gathering seaweed from the low tide area. Eliza watched as she moved farther from the shore and made several large piles of seaweed. The girl picked up a shovel and dug a deep hole in the sand. In the bottom of the hole, the girl placed some of the seaweed. Soon she walked into the forest too.

Eliza looked at her bucket and realized that she'd better get busy. She could see that the low tide was beginning to edge up to its normal level. She quickly began picking mussels from the rocks with her knife as she moved back up the beach toward her tent.

When Eliza returned with her bucket, her mother came with a washtub, and Father filled it with seawater. Then he went to Swan Lake just up the hill and brought several chunks of ice that still floated in the water. He placed the ice in the washtub.

"Now they will last us a few days," Father said. "Mussel stew, fried mussels, steamed mussels, and any other way we can learn to fix them. We'll have good eating this week. Even though we haven't had them before, I think we will like them and be thankful to God for them."

Eliza told them about the things she had seen while she'd gathered the mussels. "I didn't know what to think when that whale came up behind the canoes. I was sure it was going to jump right in."

"The whales come north when the herring run. They will follow the herring up north," Father said. "Whales love to eat herring. It sounds like the Tlingit do too."

"What do you think the white sacs on the branches are?" Eliza asked her father as she put away the lunch dishes.

"The women were gathering herring egg sacs," Father told her. "It is for food, like caviar."

Amos was in the tent napping. He coughed and choked as he struggled to breathe. Mother leaned over him, patting his back and feeling his head with her hand.

"After a week, he still has a high fever, Edvard," Mother said in a worried voice. Her face looked drawn and pinched.

Father entered the tent and stood with his wife, looking at Amos. Amos was damp from the sweat he poured out even though the air was cool. "There is no blood in what he spits up. We still have hope. We always have hope when we trust in God. Come in here, Eliza. We must pray."

As they all finished praying, Eliza heard Katrina calling up the beach. She excitedly ran out of the tent flap and waited for her friend to reach the tent.

Breathlessly, Katrina tried to speak when she arrived. "I heard from Erm. Erm's friend from the Raven Clan, Monutat, was at the Tlingit market this morning. He say he tell Erm we come."

"When can we go?" Eliza asked.

"I am free now. Could you go now?" Katrina asked eagerly.

"Where is the Tlingit market?" Father asked. "I am not familiar with the Tlingit market."

"It built in north wall of fort. We trade for things with Raven Clan. I was there this morning," Katrina told him.

"Perhaps we can trade for more food and other things we need from them. How far is Erm's village?" asked Father.

"My father say take forty-five minutes to walk to Erm's village," Katrina said.

Father told Eliza, "You may go for a couple of hours, but be back by dinner. It gets dark in that forest, especially with the sun hidden behind those dark clouds."

"Are you sure? Do you need me to stay with Amos?" Eliza asked.

"I'll be around the tent today," Father said. "I'll help with Amos. Just be careful, and don't stay too long."

"Oh, thank you, Father!" Eliza said excitedly.

CHAPTER 9

E liza followed Katrina to the trail to the Tlingit village. She told
Katrina about the things she had seen that morning. She talked
to Katrina about the Tlingit women who were gathering herring
eggs. She asked about the girl she saw gathering seaweed.

"Herring lay eggs on seaweed. Tlingit learn they lay eggs on
branches in water too," Katrina told her. "They eat all kind fish eggs.
I am not sure why girl gather seaweed. It might have eggs too."

As they neared the Tlingit village, Eliza could hear the murmur
of voices. Men were chanting and singing. It sounded as if they were
stomping the ground, making war whoops. Some men were in the
larger canoes with oars in their hands.

"What are they doing?" Eliza whispered to Katrina.

"Whale hunt," Katrina whispered back.

After the chanting and dancing, the men with harpoons leaped
into the canoes and quickly pushed them into the river. They were
silent now as they began their pursuit of the whales.

Eliza stood stock still at the end of the path from Sitka. She
began examining the village. Five very large, long houses that the
Tlingit called lodges stood in a row, set back from the shore of the
Indian River. Each house had a twelve-foot pole in front of it with
carved, brightly painted ornate animal figures, each sitting above
the other. Eliza had learned that totem pole carvings explained the
history or adventures of each house.

A huge fire had burned recently. The smell of wood smoke and damp ashes hung in the air. Rows of drying salmon fillets filled the spaces on each side of the fire pit. A strong smell of fish, damp fur, leather, and dogs mixed with the smoke and ashes. At the end of tethers, the dogs were barking fiercely and howling. Puppies danced at their feet, yipping and making high-pitched howls, imitating their parents. The sights, sounds, and smells of the Tlingit village overpowered Eliza. She began to tremble as she anticipated what would come next.

When the people noticed them, every person silently stared at her and Katrina. Small children peered around the woven reed skirts of their mothers or peeked out of the doors of the lodges.

Erm and Monutat approached the village on the path from the beach. All of the dogs were barking, but the people were silent. Katrina stood in the clearing with a strange girl with golden hair.

Monutat stepped backward and disappeared into the forest.

A Tlingit man strutted forward and spoke, "*Aaa', neil gu'?*"

To Eliza, it sounded as if he were clearing his throat and clucking his tongue. Sounds popped and erupted from his mouth.

Katrina simply said, "Erm?"

Erm quickly came to stand beside the chief.

Eliza listened intently as Erm, speaking in Tlingit, told the chief that Katrina was her friend from the girls' school. She told him she didn't know the girl with the golden hair. Then Erm turned and smiled at Katrina.

"Eliza came last month from America. I brought her here to meet you ... see your village," Katrina told Erm.

Erm translated to the chief. The chief was silent. The people whispered the news to one another. The chief continued to look at the two girls with stern dark eyes.

Eliza's mouth went dry as dread seized her. He looked so fierce. She feared he was going to throw the knife that hung at his side. He was dressed in leather pants and a lightweight parka made of seal gut. His cone-shaped hat also had an added woven cylinder shape attached to the peak. It was made of woven reeds in intricate designs. A narrow, carved, painted turtle sat on the top of the cylinder. On his chest hung a large shield made of eagle quills tied together with brightly colored strings of beads. In the center was a painted picture of a burned house with smoke coming from it. It made him look even fiercer.

"*Yak' ei*," he said as he turned abruptly and stalked away.

Katrina and Erm both reached their hands toward one another as soon as the chief welcomed Eliza and Katrina to the village. They clutched each other at the elbows. Both of them said at the same time, "It is good to see you again!"

"This is Eliza," Katrina said as she put her arm around Eliza's shoulder.

"Good," Erm said shyly. "Come, see village."

Eliza followed Katrina and Erm around the village. Erm told them about the tall totem poles in front of each lodge. She pointed to the one with a wolf carved and painted on the top. Erm explained that the wolf on the totem represented their family. She pointed out the carvings in front of other houses. One had an eagle, another, a turtle, and the other houses were represented by a salmon and a bear.

Designs similar to the totems were painted on the sides of each house built of cedar planks. Erm told them that the turtle was the most powerful house, because the chief came from the Turtle House. With Katrina's help, Erm explained that there were two main clans—the Eagle Clan and the Raven Clan. Her village was part of the Eagle Clan and was called the Burnt House Tribe.

Erm took them into her Wolf House, which sat in the middle of the five lodges. There was a large fire burning in the middle of the lodge. Above the fire was a hole in the roof to allow the smoke to escape. The fire pit was lined with stone, and the fire was built on the dirt bottom. The floor and sides of the lodge were made of cedar, which gave off the sweet aroma of the forest.

Eliza watched the women who squatted at the fire stirring a large pot. Curious, she looked around the lodge where others were sewing furs, weaving baskets or cloth from reeds, and making other needed items. Each long side of the lodge was lined with two rows of benches made from sturdy wooden poles. They looked like the bunk beds her cousins slept in back in Wisconsin. The upper bunk held fur blankets, clothes, beautiful bentwood boxes, baskets, and pots, which stored their food and other household needs. Some of the lower bunks were wider, and each bunk was covered by a large fur blanket.

Eliza watched the young children play on some of the lower benches and the floor. She smiled as she compared these children to Amos. She realized that all children must act the same. She wondered if Tlingit children fell into the sea like Amos. Her smiled faded.

She saw small leather hammocks hanging between the ends of the bunks holding sleeping babies. She tiptoed over to look into a swinging bed and smiled at the cute, round-cheeked baby with coal-black hair.

Eliza learned that Erm had seven members in her family: her mother, father, sister, her sister's husband and daughter, and their grandmother.

The other people in the lodge were her aunts, uncles, and cousins from her mother's side of the family. Erm called her cousins *brother* and *sister*, because the children of each house were considered one large common family. There were a total of twenty-four people living in the Wolf House. Each individual family's space was partitioned from the next space with animal skins.

"This is my aunt," Erm said, introducing one of the women at the fire. "She teach me things I must know to be woman."

"It is very nice to meet you," Eliza said as she smiled at the woman.

The woman nodded at her and smiled. She wore a tan dress made of woven reeds. It was decorated with all types of beadwork. She wore her hair in a short bob with bangs growing long on her forehead. Necklaces and bracelets of many colored beads, shells, and animal teeth adorned her neck, arms, and ankles. Leather moccasins in the shape of a canoe were tied to her feet with strips of leather. They were beautifully decorated with beads and painted pictures.

As they left Erm's house, Eliza wondered why Erm didn't introduce them to her mother. Eliza had many questions for Erm.

"Why did you have such a big fire here?" Eliza asked.

"We had salmon ... um ..." Erm paused.

"Drums, dance, and sing?" asked Katrina.

"Yes," replied Erm.

"They had a salmon party or celebration," said Katrina.

"Why do they have a salmon celebration?" asked Eliza.

"Not many salmon," Erm said. "We dance, salmon come back."

"Why aren't there as many salmon?" asked Eliza.

"Salmon cannery," Erm replied.

Katrina told Eliza, "More Americans come now. They build factory to can salmon. They take many salmon."

"Come, I show you," Erm said, walking to a path to the sea.

The girls walked through the thick forest. When they reached the shore, they turned left and walked through a clump of thick cedar trees. Finally, they came to a clearing. Across the river stood a large building with a sign that read Indian River Salmon Cannery. The smell of rotting fish permeated the air and caused Eliza's stomach to roll. She took her cotton hankie from her apron pocket and covered her nose and mouth with it.

Eliza could see men running back and forth from a platform that was built out over the river. They filled baskets with salmon that the cannery's nets had trapped in the river. Each man carried two baskets hung on a pole that they laid across their shoulders. Water drained out of the baskets' loose weave as they ran stooped over toward the large building.

An English-speaking man shouted instructions, urging them to hurry. The men ran from the platform, dumped the salmon into big bins, and ran back again. When the bins were full, other men picked them up and carried them into the building. Still other men came from a door in the back of the building. They dumped fish heads and guts into the river to be carried out to the sea.

"I've seen men like that before. They were all over the wharf at San Francisco!" exclaimed Eliza.

"Chinese come," informed Katrina. "They help owners can salmon up and down the coast. The Russian-American Company sell to people in America. Our ships took them to Fort Ross in California. Fort Ross closed now. They take to San Francisco now."

Erm put her hands on her hips. "Now, no salmon come upriver for Tlingit. Tlingit afraid we not have food for winter."

Katrina said, "The Tlingit tried to get Russian government to protect the fishing grounds. Six years ago, Tlingit attack Russian fort. Many Tlingit killed. Russia make new laws, no protect Tlingit. Tlingit not like Russians. Russians afraid of Tlingit. But not Erm. We be friends. Americans come. Some nice; some not."

"The Americans and some Russians watch over our village," Erm said. "We not afraid of warring tribes in the north."

"Erm's village help us get food," Katrina said.

As the girls turned to head back to the village, Katrina put her arm around Erm's shoulders. They walked, quietly lost in their thoughts. Suddenly, Erm whispered, "Stop," as she stared ahead through the trees. "Quiet."

Leaves were rustling. Twigs broke as something crashed through the bushes. There was strange snorting and groaning. All three girls froze. A large brown bear lumbered onto the path about fifty feet in front of them. The bear stood on his hind legs and let out a loud growl and then shook his massive head back and forth. He towered above the girls, making them feel small and defenseless. The bear let out another loud growl as he stood there swaying.

"No move, no sound." Erm whispered as she stood up as tall as she could and raised her arms. "Get big, stay close."

CHAPTER 10

The bear seemed to sense that an enemy was nearby. His beady eyes squinted as he tried to understand what was ahead of him. He came down on all fours and swung his head back and forth.

Eliza and Katrina pressed their bodies up as close as they could to Erm. They put their hands up too, touching Erm's hands to make themselves look like a large animal.

In a deep, firm, but quiet voice, Erm spoke to the bear in Tlingit. "Brother Bear, do not be afraid. I am your friend. Long ago, you were my brother. Your spirit lives in me."

The bear shook his massive head again, cocked his ears, and looked intently for the soft voice. He stood on his hind feet again, roaring. He shook his head up and down several times, making huffing sounds. The bear came down on all four feet, grunting and snorting. He made deep claw marks in the dirt path.

"Stop where you are. You go your way, and we will go ours," Erm continued.

The bear stood again, swaying and grunting for what seemed like a long time. Finally, he came down on all fours. He swung his head from side to side.

"May your fishing be good," Erm whispered.

The bear turned his head and took a powerful lunge into the brush and lumbered into the forest toward the river. The girls remained still until Erm said it was all right to move. They could hear the bear splashing the water of the river.

Eliza let her breath out with a whoosh. Her heart still beat as if she had just run a hundred miles. Her arms felt like lead as she dropped them to her side.

"How did you do that? Have you done that before?" asked Eliza when she could speak.

"No, never before. The bear ... brother, I talk him. He listen. Bear not smart," Erm replied as if she had done nothing out of the ordinary. "My aunt said three things to do when see bear. Run—be killed. Climb tree—maybe live. Stand still, make self big—live."

Eliza just stared at Erm. She couldn't believe she could be so brave. "Why do you say the bear is your brother?"

"Long ago, all things Raven make are brothers. The trees, plants, salmon, deer, birds, all things," Erm said as she pointed to each of the girls. "My brothers talk together like us."

Eliza could not imagine talking to a tree. That didn't make sense. She had learned that God created all things. A raven was just a bird. How could a bird create the world?

As they passed the sand beach, Eliza noticed a big rock sitting on a piece of wood lying in the sand. She asked, "Why is that stone sitting on that piece of wood?"

"Make *k'ink'*," Erm said.

"Stink heads," Katrina said, making a face. "Put salmon heads in hole. They rot. Tlingit think good to eat. Very bad."

"Yes," said Erm as she rubbed her stomach. "Good!"

Eliza's stomach turned a bit. She had just learned what rotting fish smelled like.

"I saw a girl on the beach this morning when I gathered mussels," Eliza said.

"That me. I need seaweed. Make *k'ink'*," Erm said. "I put seaweed, salmon heads, and seawater in hole. They sit all summer. Ready when get cold."

Eliza looked at Katrina. "Eew! I see what you mean."

"Katrina, I tell you secret," Erm said.

"What is it?" Katrina asked.

"Monutat come. He help me. He tell me I strong woman." Erm said, smiling. "I think he like me. I know him two years. He come see me many time. I think he handsome. I like him much."

Eliza and Katrina stared gaping at her.

After a pause, Erm said, "His uncle will ask my aunt if he can marry me. We wait."

"How old are you?" Eliza asked.

"I thirteen summers. Monutat twenty summers. Time for man to marry," Erm said. "Monutat good hunter."

"You are too young!" Eliza exclaimed.

"Girl marry when be woman," Erm said.

Eliza realized that would mean she was old enough to marry in the Tlingit culture. Erm probably thought she and Katrina were old maids.

When they arrived back at Erm's village, several people were gathered outside singing or chanting.

"What is happening?" asked Eliza.

"Shaman," Erm replied.

"What is a shaman? And what is he doing?" asked Eliza.

Erm turned and asked a woman what was happening. The woman told Erm in Tlingit that Yeikoo'shk' was ill. He had been shouting loudly and had fallen down many times. He was invaded by evil spirits, and the shaman was driving them out.

Eliza had heard of evil spirits. They were talked about in the Bible. Jesus could cast out evil spirits, but Eliza had never heard of a shaman. How could a man cast out evil spirits?

At that moment, the chanting and drums stopped. From the door of the Salmon House emerged a man wearing a painted wooden mask. It was mostly red with black slashes for eyebrows and hair. The areas around the eyes were painted green, and a long, red wooden tongue hung from the hole for the mouth. The shaman's clothes were torn and muddy; his hair was long and stringy. A worn red blanket with totem figures woven into the fabric covered his shoulders. His eyes searched the gathered crowd. He pointed his spear at several people and shouted out in Tlingit.

Screaming and leaping into the air, the shaman pointed his spear at Eliza and Katrina. Then he ran straight at them, continuing to shout with his spear raised. Erm slowly stepped back. Compared to when Erm talked to the bear, she didn't seem so brave to Eliza when she was faced with the shaman.

CHAPTER 11

Eliza and Katrina ducked behind Erm as the shaman skidded to a stop in front of them. He shook his rattles and waved the spear. Then he stomped his feet and shouted strange words at Erm. Erm bowed her head. Immediately, the shaman turned and ran into the dense cedar trees of the forest.

The people stared at Eliza and then went back to their work. Their curiosity was satisfied.

Finally, Eliza whispered, "Why did the shaman do that? What did he say?"

"He say you and Katrina bring evil spirits to village. If you come back, he say he going to make spirits come out."

Both Eliza and Katrina gasped.

"Why shaman stop?" asked Katrina.

Looking at Eliza, Erm answered, "He say you have very powerful spirit. It say leave you alone."

"I have the Spirit of God in me. God is the most powerful Spirit in the world," Eliza whispered. "I think God protected me because He has more for me to do."

Katrina looked at Eliza strangely. "I know of God, but He cannot be in you. He only in heaven, far, far away."

"Yes, God is in heaven, but He sends His Spirit to live in everyone who believes that Jesus died for their sins. God's Spirit is a good and powerful Spirit. God's Spirit helps me to decide on the right things to do and guides and protects me," Eliza said with wonder. "Even from a shaman."

"Shaman very strong spirit," Erm said. "Your spirit be very strong!"

"My God is the Almighty Spirit. He has authority over all spirits," Eliza said.

"He rule over bear and shaman spirits?" Erm asked.

"I believe He does," Eliza said.

A call came from the door of the Wolf House. "Eat. You come?" asked Erm.

"Yes," said Katrina. "I am hungry. It take time to get home."

Once inside, Erm led them to her area of the lodge. Erm introduced them to her family. "Mother," she said as a woman came toward them with wooden bowls of steaming food. Erm's mother handed Eliza and Katrina a bowl and a spoon made from the horn of a mountain sheep. Eliza turned the spoon over and over, looking at how it was made and beautifully carved. The curve at the base of the horn was used as the bowl of the spoon. The upper side of the horn had been cut off. The handle was cut to be thin enough to hold comfortably in a hand and ended at the curved tip of the horn. Delicate carvings of Tlingit art adorned the bowl and up the handle. The carvings of animals reminded Eliza of the figures on the totem poles outside the houses.

As Erm's mother returned to bring other bowls from the common pot on the fire, Eliza looked at her bowl. "Dear Lord, I don't know what this is, but thank You for this food and my new friends," she whispered.

"What are you saying?" asked Katrina.

"I'm thanking God for our food," Eliza said.

"Wait, 'til after you eat," Katrina laughed.

Eliza noticed shells in her bowl, along with other chunks of meat. Green stringy things were floating in it too. She took one of the shells out, wondering what she would do with it. Then she noticed that Erm had taken one too. Erm put it to her mouth, pulled something from the shell with her teeth, and then tossed the shell into a big bowl on the floor.

Eliza looked closely at the shell. She could see that there was a morsel of food in it. She slid the food into her mouth and started to chew. It felt as if she were eating dirt. It crunched and felt grainy in her mouth. The outside was slimy and tasted salty. She wasn't sure what to do with it, so she swallowed it down without chewing anymore.

Eliza picked at the stew with her spoon and fished out what looked like a chunk of fish. She liked the fish and ate all of the chunks she could find. Then she decided to try the stringy green stuff. It kept sliding off her spoon, but finally she was able to get some into her mouth. It was tough and slimy. It tasted like the rotting fish smelled. She could not chew it, so she swallowed it whole. As the stringy mass slithered down, the salty taste irritated her throat, and she began to cough.

Eliza glanced around at the others who were eating the stew with relish. She noticed that even Katrina was enjoying the meal.

"What is in this?" she asked Erm.

"It made from oysters, cod, and seaweed," Erm said. "It my favorite."

As the family ate, they talked and laughed, just like her family. Erm's niece was just learning to walk and reminded Eliza of Amos when he was that age. Eliza could tell that mealtime was a time when this family shared its news and enjoyed each other's company. Eliza watched Erm's grandmother as she held the baby. The act reminded Eliza of her own grandmother back in Wisconsin when she played with Amos. Eliza yearned to be with her family again. Although the lodge was crowded, Eliza thought it would be great to live together with her aunts, uncles, and cousins.

Suddenly, Erm said, "It get late. Darkness comes fast. It far to Sitka. My father say you go now."

Walking to the path to Sitka, Katrina asked, "Are you coming to school? It start on Monday next. That ten more days."

"Yes, I come. I be happy to see my friends," Erm said. "My friend Monutat be there. He go boys' seminary at bishop's house."

"We must hurry!" Eliza said. "I didn't know so much time had passed. My father said to only stay for a couple of hours."

As Eliza and Katrina hurried down the path, they talked about all that they had seen and done that day. They were so intent on sharing their thoughts that they didn't notice how dark it was getting in the deep forest.

There had been heavy, dark clouds in the sky all day. Now Eliza couldn't even see the sky because of the tall cedars and pine trees. Rain began to patter on the leaves and drip from the thick tree limbs above. The wind from the sea blew through the trees, making an eerie sound as if hundreds of snakes were hanging in the trees, hissing and rattling their tails. The smell of moss and damp rotting wood filled Eliza's nostrils.

Eliza could hear thumps, rustling, crunching, and swishing sounds from the dark forest. The long hoot of an owl and the snake sounds of the swishing branches continued to fill the night air. Twigs being blown from the trees made pops and eerie sounds when they tumbled to the ground around them. Howls from a pack of wolves sent shivers down Eliza's back. Other smaller animals made thrashing sounds in the bushes near the path. Shadows flitted over the path as the wind blustered through the trees. She didn't know what could be out there. Was it the bear?

"Did you hear that?" Katrina asked, grabbing Eliza's arm.

"What?" whispered Eliza as she strained to listen.

The darkness continued to crowd in. The sound of rattling disturbed the darkness. "Do you think it is the shaman coming to get us?" asked Eliza.

CHAPTER 12

—⁓∾⊙⊙⊙⊙∾⁓—

"I don't know what it is," Katrina whispered back as she grabbed Eliza's hand. A loud grunt drew their attention to the other side of the path.

"Let's run," said Eliza.

They started off running, but soon Eliza heard a loud thud on the path behind her. The sound of cloth and shoes dragging across the ground filled Eliza's ears. Then Katrina cried out.

Panicking, Eliza stopped and called, "Katrina, are you still here?"

She heard Katrina quietly sniffling. "What happened?" asked Eliza as she began to walk carefully toward Katrina's voice in the gray darkness.

"I fall on roots. My knee bleed. Not hurt. But tore dress," Katrina sobbed. "This my only day dress. Meti be very, very angry. I must take care my dress, she say."

"We need to get home. Can you walk?" Eliza asked.

"Yes, can walk," Katrina said.

Eliza tried to look around. "I think we need to pray."

"Father Iakov say only priests can pray," Katrina whispered.

"We can say prayers to God at any time," said Eliza. "God hears our prayers each time we pray." Eliza bowed her head and prayed, "Dear Father in heaven, please help us get home. Guide us and protect us from the things in this forest. In Jesus's name, amen."

The night sounds of the forest continued to press in on all sides. Walking quickly, the girls stumbled over the rocks and roots in the path. Katrina walked forward toward Sitka. She kept looking back and forth to see if she could see what was ahead making the noises in the forest. Eliza walked behind her facing backward, watching to see if someone or something was following them. She hung on to the skirt of Katrina's dress. They heard the yipping and the long lonely howling of wolves in the distance. An owl made its haunting hooting sound from a swaying branch nearby. The path snaked back and forth as it went around moss-covered trees and fallen logs.

Suddenly, they heard grunting and rustling leaves from their right. Eliza and Katrina scanned the forest for what could be making the sounds. As they moved slowly forward, Katrina bumped into something tall and hard. Eliza bumped into Katrina at the sudden stop. Both girls screamed.

"I'm sorry," a deep voice said.

A faint light bobbed to the right of them. It was moving back and forth. Then someone bellowed out among the trees. The girls looked back and forth from the man to the swinging light coming toward them.

"Take it easy, Ben," said the man on the path. "You're scaring these nice young ladies to death."

"Ladies? Didn't know we had ladies here 'bouts." When he reached the path, he said, "Oh, I know this little one. Visited her tent a while back." Ben slurred as he touched Eliza's face. "Been keeping my eye on her. By the way, how's that little brother of yours?"

"He's very sick. The doctor came again this morning," Eliza said. "He gave us some more medicine."

"Aw, he's a fake. Don't count on him," Ben replied. "Russian doctors are worse than those butchers they had sawing off good men's arms on the battlefield in the Civil War. I was glad when that war was over. Came here to seek my fortune."

The young man's voice was stern but gentle. "Leave her alone. You have no right to be bothering her. She is the new reverend's daughter, and you should not be touching her. And don't go scaring them with horror tales from the war. You go on back home, Ben. Take the lantern so you don't get off the path."

Eliza clung to Katrina as the old miner stumbled down the path, swaying as he went, mumbling all the way. They peered at the young man as the light faded away.

Without the lantern, Eliza couldn't see the young man clearly. His face was completely in the shadows. As her eyes became used to the dark, she could see that he was slim and muscular. He didn't look much older than Katrina. His voice was gentle as he reassured the girls in the darkness. Eliza was sure that he must be kind.

"Come with me. I will see you ladies home," he said as he took Eliza and Katrina by the arms. "I know this path like the back of my hand. I use it to go up to where I'm looking for gold above the Tlingit village on the Indian River. The Tlingit have been very friendly with the Americans who have come."

As they came into the lights of the fires at the tent village, Eliza glanced at Katrina's face as they walked. Eliza was puzzled by the look in Katrina's eyes as she gazed at the young man's face in ecstatic bliss. Eliza looked away, troubled.

The young man escorted Eliza to her tent. She remained silent as she watched the man and Katrina walk into the darkness.

Eliza heard her father praying as she made her way to the front of her tent. As her foot scraped on the stones outside, her father exploded from the tent flap, grabbed her, and hugged her in relief. He called out his thanks to the young miner for bringing her safely home. Eliza knew she would be in for a scolding.

"We gave you permission to go to the Tlingit village with Katrina, but we expected you back long before it got dark," Mother scolded as a final sliver of red sun sank beneath the passing dark rain clouds. Then the sun completely disappeared into the inky black sea behind her mother.

"I am sorry, Mother and Father," Eliza said. "Erm told us to leave, and we thought we would get home before it got so dark. You won't believe the things I saw and did today!"

Eliza told them about the village, the cannery, the bear, the shaman, and the food. Her parents' faces went from laughter to concern as her story unfolded. She was hoping they would forget she had stayed so late.

Amos lay on her parents' bed wrapped in blankets. Eliza could hear his deep cough that had rattled his chest for weeks now. Eliza realized that her mother didn't have help with him all day. Father had been meeting with men around Sitka each day, inviting them to church. Not only was Amos sick, but her mother also looked so weary and tired.

"Father, I want to ask you about the shaman. Do you know about them? Erm said they heal people and cast out evil spirits. Can they do that?" asked Eliza. "Could he make Amos well?"

"There are many kinds of spirits, both good and bad. I don't know what a shaman would do to heal people, but I have heard that they cast out the evil spirits of their people," Father said. "I have read that the shaman lives alone in the forest. He uses plants and other things that they say give him visions that direct him to heal or to cast out demons or evil spirits. The Tlingit believe in a spirit world, where each living thing has a spirit. Some of the spirits are good, but they fear the many spirits they believe are evil. Because of their openness to spirits, the Tlingit are often troubled by bad or evil spirits."

"If they already have belief in these spirits, how will we be able to teach them about God?"

"To understand how to share Christ with them, I hope to learn more about their beliefs and the practices of the shaman. I do not believe he could really heal Amos. We must not judge them harshly. We need to understand what they believe and why. We are asked to love them, not judge them."

After a few moments of silence, Mother said, "Your father talked to Father Iakov, and we decided to let you go to the girls' school this summer. It will give you an opportunity to learn about the Russian Orthodox religion as well as learn about the Tlingit. You will be able to help the other girls with their English and perhaps share your faith with them," Mother told her.

"Oh, thank you!" Eliza said as she hugged her parents. "I want to learn all I can about the things Katrina and Erm believe. Hopefully, I can share with them what I believe too."

"That will be good for you so that you understand their cultures more. We cannot make them change their ways of worship. The Orthodox hold to the traditions of their church more than they follow God's word. The Tlingit worship the spirits of nature. Our goal is to direct their worship only toward the God of Creation. But for now, you are required to stay at the tent to help your mother and tend to Amos for the next week. There will be no outings for you until I see that you can be responsible to your mother and family," Father said sternly as he sent her into the tent to prepare for bed.

Eliza lay in bed listening to Amos's cough. Silently, she prayed, "Please, God, make Amos well again. I'm sorry I wasn't watching him more closely the morning he went into the water. I was supposed to be watching him, but I got so wrapped up in what I wanted to be doing and in talking to Katrina. I find it so hard to fulfill my responsibilities. I know that Mother is overworked, and both of my parents are so worried about Amos. I didn't mean to worry them too by being gone so late. I just wasn't thinking. Please help me to think of others like You want me to do. I want to be helpful and good, but it's so hard when there are so many exciting things to learn and do. I pray that You will heal Amos too. In Jesus's name, amen."

As Eliza drifted into an exhausted sleep, she saw Amos in a dream, sitting on the lap of Jesus Christ.

CHAPTER 13

E liza slowly washed the dishes and put them away on Sunday morning. Being restricted to the tent for seven days was becoming wearisome. This morning, she would be staying home to care for Amos while her parents conducted the first Sunday church meeting on the rise above the town. Eliza wondered how many would come to the meeting. Would Katrina and her family be there? Maybe Erm would even come, and Eliza would miss it all.

Eliza pondered what she had learned from her visit to the Tlingit village. She had been considering the different atmosphere in her home compared to Erm's home. Although both she and Erm lived in primitive conditions, there was a very different feeling in her home and family than in Erm's village. There was more peace and fewer concerns. Although they were worried about Amos, her family knew that God was watching out for him. This gave them more peace about Amos's condition. It seemed the Tlingit worried about the salmon and where they would get their food. The shaman was so frightful, and she realized the power he had over the people. It seemed that they feared their god, while God gave her family security. She thought about how the houses and tribes were afraid that they might make another clan or the northern tribes angry and have to go to war. Why were they so worried that they wouldn't be able to live up to the expectations for their potlatch ceremonies and what each family was required to give for weddings and funerals?

Eliza knew that her home was filled with love, caring, and understanding. She did not fear any of the things that Erm and her people feared. She knew that God would take care of all of the things she needed. Her town in Wisconsin was small, but the people were not afraid of the people in other towns. They accepted each other, and expectations were not those that would lead to war. Sometimes there were disagreements, but they didn't lead to any kind of battle.

The rough men in the tent city were sometimes frightening, but in the last few weeks, she had learned not to be so afraid of them. As her father had gotten to know them, they deferred to her and her family. She had gotten to know the other members of the tent city on the ship, and she did not fear them. All of them were friends and were probably at the Sunday meeting now.

Amos was tied to Eliza's long apron strings as she worked. She was not going to take the chance that he would get away from her this morning. Amos was no longer the spunky little boy he had been six weeks ago. Now he usually sat quietly playing with his horse, looking at his Bible book, or sucking his thumb. When he tried to walk or run around in the tent, he would end up having a terrible coughing fit. He was weak and slept most of the time.

Eliza was relieved that Amos was a little better than he was a few weeks ago, but tears came to her eyes as she watched him struggle. Would he ever return to being a spunky, happy little boy? When Eliza had asked God to heal Amos, she expected God to make him a spunky, active, happy little boy, not this sad little waif. What more could she do for God so that He would heal Amos completely?

Eliza finished the chores that her mother had left for her to do. She took an empty, clean medicine bottle and filled it half full with warm water. She put leftover porridge into the bottle and put her finger over the small opening, shaking it until the porridge was mixed smoothly into the liquid. To this, she added two drops of medicine from a new bottle and shook it again. Eliza took the clean rubber nipple that they had brought from Wisconsin; it was the only way to get the medicine and food down. Amos turned his head away when they tried to feed him with a spoon. He gagged on even the softest foods. She stretched the bottom of the nipple and slipped it onto the small opening of the medicine bottle.

Sitting cross-legged on her parents' bed, she cuddled Amos into her arms and offered him the bottle. As he ate, he looked intently into Eliza's face as if to plead with her to make him feel better.

"Dear God," Eliza prayed. "Do I need to do more for You before You will heal Amos completely? Or is there some other way that Amos will be healed? Please let me understand what I need to do or some sign of how You will heal him. I know that if we pray, You hear our prayers and answer them. Help me to see Your answer. In Jesus's name, amen."

As Eliza rocked Amos, she could hear the people who came to the church meeting on the hill singing hymns. Her father's clear tenor voice drifted on the breeze. She could hear the wispy sound of the air organ that her mother played to accompany the singing. Eliza remembered the excitement when Father was able to borrow the old organ from the bishop's house.

As she listened, Eliza knew that her mother would be pumping the pedals firmly and quickly so that air would pass through the small pipes inside a wooden box attached to the keyboard. Each key was attached to a flap on each pipe. As her mother pressed the keys, the flaps would open, and the air would blow through the pipes, making a sound. The lower notes were mellow, but the higher notes sounded more like tin whistles than an accompaniment for hymns.

Eliza began to sing the hymn quietly as she rocked Amos.

> Through many dangers, toils and snares …
> We have already come.
> T'was Grace that brought us safe thus far …
> And Grace will lead us home.

Amos's eyes slowly closed, and Eliza gently laid him on the bed. She covered him with his light blanket as she quietly hummed the next verse.

The air in the tent became warm as the sun climbed higher in the sky. Eliza stepped outside and sat on the rock near the open tent flap. She shaded her eyes as she looked out over the sea. It was one of the few clear days since arriving in Sitka. The June sky was blue instead of gray, and the clouds were white and fluffy instead of the thin gray clouds that normally covered the sky. Eliza could barely distinguish the horizon as the blue of the sky faded into the blue of the sea.

Other than the distant sound of her father's voice, it was completely quiet on the beach. Small waves lapped at the rocks on the shore. Not a miner or settler was at their tent. A few Aleuts roamed about; others had gone to the Orthodox church. The dogs slept in the sun. What a beautiful, peace-filled day. Eliza wished she could capture that feeling forever. Who could she share this peaceful moment with?

Eliza rose and entered the tent. She looked through her trunk and found the box of paper her grandmother had sent with her with instructions to write to her. Now seemed the perfect time to write. With paper, pen, and ink, Eliza returned to the rock and began writing.

> *Dear Grandmother,*
>
> *It is beautiful here in Sitka. The mountaintops are still covered with snow even in June. Below the snow, the mountains are covered with deep green cedar and pine trees that come down to meet the blue sea. Now the breeze is gentle and becoming warm. It is not like the bitter cold, damp wind that stormed into the shore when we first arrived. It rained almost every day when we first got here.*

Eliza wrote about meeting Katrina and Erm. She wrote about her new parka and Erm's village. She wanted her grandmother to know how generous and kind her new friends were. Eliza told about the bear and all of the things she was doing and learning.

This week, I will be able to go to the girls' school that teaches English to the Russian and Tlingit girls. Father Iakov, the teacher at the bishop's house, wants me to help to teach correct English. Katrina's and Erm's English has improved already in the six weeks we have been talking.

Today is the first church meeting Father has been able to hold. I am missing it, because I have had such a hard time being good and helping Mother. I seem to have no self-control and just run off to do things instead of helping her. Mother always lets me go, but I know she would rather I stay to help her or take care of Amos. Then I get so caught up in the things I am doing and learning about that I forget the time.

I know that Father has written you about Amos. I feel so guilty about how sick he is. I was right there on the beach when it happened. I was talking to Katrina instead of keeping an eye on him. He is still very sick with a terrible cough, and he seems so tired all of the time. Even the medicine does not seem to help. Please pray to God that Amos will be well again.

Sometimes I get so confused. I let Amos get sick, I worry Mother and Father, and I wander off when I should be helping them with the mission. I wonder sometimes if the shaman I saw in Erm's village cast a spell on me that makes me disobey. I know all of the things I should do, but I don't do them. Katrina has such a kind heart and obeys her mother so much more than I do my mother. Erm's religion seems to make

her so brave. I am not obedient, helpful, generous, or
brave. What has my God and faith made me? I wish
I could talk to you about all of these things. I am
so mixed up. I know you could help me understand
how God is working in my life. Please pray for me to
know how to be the good person I know God wants
me to be.

With love, hugs, and kisses,
Eliza

Eliza folded her letter. In her small, neat handwriting, she wrote her Grandmother's address on the smooth side. Then she got out the small rod of red sealing wax. She heated one end of it over the coals of the cook fire and dropped three drops of sealing wax onto the place where the four sides of the folded letter met on the back. She pressed the metal stamp with the letter *H* engraved on it into the sealing wax. A perfect *H* appeared in the middle of the red blob of wax on the letter. She blew on it so that the wax would harden and seal her letter.

As Eliza thought about her letter to Grandmother, a tear formed in her eye. She had always thought of herself as obedient, yet it no longer seemed that she was. She had only obeyed resentfully when asked to do things by her mother. Throughout the Bible, she knew God asked her to have faith and obey willingly. She shivered in spite of the warmth of the sun. Eliza folded her hands and bent over until her head touched her knees. She sobbed uncontrollably until she heard Amos's hoarse cry and his uncontrollable cough.

CHAPTER 14

B efore school started on Monday, Eliza gathered wood from the edge of the forest and the beach.

Walking noiselessly up behind her, Erm asked, "I help?"

"Erm, you scared me!" Eliza said as she dropped the wood she had gathered.

"You drop mouth and wood," Erm teased.

Giggling, the girls picked up the wood again.

"Are you on your way to school?" asked Eliza as they walked back toward her tent.

"Yes," said Erm.

"Oh, Mother, look who's here," Eliza called as they neared the tent. "I want you to meet Erm." Eliza carefully stacked the wood she had gathered on the woodpile.

Mrs. Healy came to the tent flap with Amos on her hip. Eliza noticed the usual pesky wisp of hair fluttering about her mother's face. It was thin and dull now. Her mother's faded cotton work dress hung loosely on her thin body. She gave the largest portions of food to Father and her and would eat only a little. Her eyes looked tired, yet her smile was as bright as ever. Eliza was worried about her mother. With the work to keep the family clothed and fed and a very sick baby, her mother's desire to serve the women in the camp and town was taking its toll. She taught a Bible study twice a week and helped the other women in the camp with laundry and child care and other ways she could serve. Eliza was concerned that her mother would become ill too.

Eliza's mother greeted Erm warmly as she extended her hand. "Erm, it is so nice to finally meet you."

Erm had a puzzled look on her face as she bowed her head toward Mrs. Healy.

"Oh, I forgot. Tlingit do not shake hands," Mrs. Healy said. "Are you walking to school with Eliza today? It will be so nice for her not to have to go alone."

Erm nodded.

"Do you need me to do anything else before I go?" asked Eliza.

"I know you need to hurry on to school, Erm, but I hope you can stop by sometime so we can get to know each other," Mrs. Healy said. Turning to Eliza, she nodded her head.

"I would like to mail my letter to Grandmother. May I have a penny to buy some stamps at the general store after school?"

"You may go, but you must come right home afterward," Mother said as she dug a penny from her purse.

"I go with you," Erm said. She held up a leather bag. "My aunt asked me to trade this dried salmon for cloth at store. It soft, not like woven reed cloth. Feel," Erm said as she held her skirt out to Eliza. "I have a deerskin dress too."

"This cloth is rough, like the denim cloth Mr. Strauss's company makes for miners' pants in America," Eliza said. "Sort of stiff but very tough and durable. I can see why your mother would like to use softer cloth."

"Then come right home afterward," her mother reminded her.

Eliza and Erm walked by the front of the bishop's house on their way to the girls' school near the back wall of the fort. Eliza was surprised to see so many young men standing in the yard waiting for school to begin. Eliza's father had told her that the bishop's house not only housed the school and seminary on the first floor but that Bishop Innocent and the priests who served in Sitka lived on the second floor.

The bishop's house and the governor's house on Castle Hill were very similar. They were the size of two or three houses put together in Wisconsin. Large logs cut with flat twelve-inch sides were used for the construction of the house. The bishop's house was painted yellow with eleven large windows on the upper floor and nine windows, plus two large doors on the lower floor. Black shutters, which could be closed to keep out the cold in the winter, framed each window.

Eliza spotted Katrina coming to meet them. Her dark hair was piled neatly on her head, and she looked lovely. A tall, dark-haired boy stood next to her. In a way, he looked familiar. Then he smiled.

"Is that Katrina's brother?" Eliza whispered to Erm as they made their way toward Katrina.

"Yes, Maxim. We say Max," Erm said as they approached Katrina and Max.

"Hello," said Katrina as she hugged both Eliza and Erm. The tall dark boy stared at Eliza.

"*Allo*, Erm. Who is this?" Max asked with a toss of his head in Eliza's direction.

"This is American girl I talk about. Her name is Eliza," Katrina answered. "We went to Erm's village together."

"*Allo*," Max said with a twinkle in his eye. "One more girl to trick."

"Do not mind him. Remember I say he big headache," Katrina said as she took Erm and Eliza by the hands, moving them on.

All of the children turned as the noise of one of the two large doors at the front of the bishop's house groaned open. Standing on the steps was a tall, thin man wearing a long black robe. Over his shoulders, golden strips of cloth ran diagonally across his chest, meeting in the middle. On his head sat a tall, round black hat with no brim. He rang his bell and told the boys and young Tlingit men to come in.

Russian boys entered by the door on the left, and the Tlingit boys entered the school through the door on the right. Max quickly ran and grabbed Eliza's arm and began dragging her toward the open door.

"Let me go!" she shouted as she struggled to get loose.

Max let go of her arm so quickly that Eliza fell backward onto the ground. With a smirk and a laugh, he walked to the door. He glanced over his shoulder at Eliza as she stood up and brushed her dress off. Eliza glared at him and stuck out her tongue.

"Come quickly, Eliza. Don't mind him. He is a pain and make trouble. Are you all right?" asked Katrina, taking Eliza by the hand and pulling her up the street.

The girls' school was at the rear of the fort, built against the stockades. It was a long climb, passing by the ship being built at the shipyard, the Russian barracks, and the Russian cemetery. The school was little more than a shack with a sagging porch and overhang.

Eliza climbed the two steps to the porch. The boards of the porch creaked as she walked across them. They seemed to bounce a little as she stepped on them. She entered the first room, which was lit by one window and the open door. Benches were placed in rows down the center of the room. The girls were seated on a bench by their ages. Eliza, Katrina, and Erm sat on the last bench, since they were the oldest girls.

As the girls settled, Eliza looked around the room. Most of the girls were dressed in Tlingit dresses. They were made of reed cloth similar to that of Erm's dress. The dresses were shorter than Eliza's dress, coming just below the knees. The top of the dresses hung straight from the shoulders until they reached the middle of the girls' thighs. The lower part of their dresses was gathered so that a ruffle completed the length of the dress. Where the bodice met the ruffle there was beautifully embroidered, beaded, or decorated trim. The same trim surrounded the neck and sometimes the sleeves, making cuffs. Narrow pants could be seen between the hem and the fur mukluks or leather shoes they wore on their feet.

There were two or three younger girls who were dressed in the Russian style. Their dresses were white and made much like Eliza's dress. She now noticed that Katrina wore the same type of white dress. Eliza guessed that it must be the uniform Russian girls wore to school.

Eliza glanced at her own dress. She only had four dresses—a homespun dress she did her work in, two calico dresses, and her gray linsey-woolsey, which was packed away for the summer. Her newer calico dress was for Sunday, and she wore her older calico dress to school. Since she would need to wear it all week, she wore an apron to protect it from wear and to keep it clean. She had enough aprons for each day of the week, so she could wear a clean one each day.

The room was very bare, with one bookcase along the wall with a few books and a pile of slates for writing. Then Eliza noticed a quiet whisper and rustling sound. It grew louder as Eliza heard footsteps on the porch outside. Father Iakov ducked his head as he entered through the door. His long black robe swished from side to side as he walked, making the quiet rustling sound. He stopped for a moment at the front of the room. Then he began to talk in a thin, quiet voice, his hands clasped behind his back.

CHAPTER 15

⟶⟿⟿⟿⟿

"Welcome to zee first day of summer school. I hope you vill learn much these few months," Father Iakov said. "I know you vill vork very hard to do vell." He looked about the room, and then his eyes came to rest upon Eliza. He slowly began to walk to the back of the room. "I see ve have a new girl in our class this summer." As he leaned over Katrina, the ends of his beautifully embroidered belt fell to within inches of Eliza's face. It appeared that his waist was encircled by beautiful, bright red roses.

Eliza looked shyly up into the priest's face. His face seemed kind, but his height caused him to loom over her.

"Are you zee American girl?" he asked.

"*Yah*, sir," Eliza whispered, reverting to the Swedish word.

Father Iakov threw his head back, laughing at Eliza's reaction. "I talk to your father. He say you can teach the children, *da*? I think your name is Miss Healy."

"My name is Eliza Healy," she said. "I didn't think I would actually be teaching the children, only helping. I thought there would be a real teacher in the room."

"How old are you?" Father Iakov asked.

"I will be fifteen in November," she replied.

"Old enough. You vill be called Miss Healy, and you vill be teaching the younger girls," Father Iakov said as he returned to the front of the class.

"Front row, show Miss Healy to your classroom," he said.

"Eliza, you must go. You must obey what Father Iakov say," Katrina whispered to her.

Eight small girls stood up and marched to the room in the back of the school. Each step they took echoed on the wide wooden boards and matched the beat of Eliza's heart. She slowly followed them, not knowing what to think or how she could teach them.

When Eliza entered the classroom, she realized that it must have been a storage room. It was small and dark. All of the girls were sitting down primly on two benches in the middle of the room, their hands in their laps.

Eliza walked by the small table and chair placed at the front of the room. She noticed that a portion of the front wall of the room was painted black. She ran her hand along the smooth, worn surface of the table. Two large pieces of chalk and many small ones, a wet cloth, and a small container of water sat on the table. Next to them lay eight slates. Eliza turned and stared at the girls, and they stared back expectantly.

Clearing her throat, Eliza said, "Good morning." The students stared back at her. Eliza tried again. "Hello."

A small, quiet voice whispered, "Hello."

Eliza looked at the girl. "Yes, yes, very good."

The little girl's face lit up into a big smile.

Eliza said hello again and again until all of the girls attempted to say it. Eliza smiled at them as their pronunciation improved. Pointing to herself, she said, "My name is Miss Healy." Pointing to the little girl who had first said hello, Eliza asked, "What is your name?"

Again there was silence. The little girl who had spoken before stood up and walked over to Eliza. The girl's shiny black hair was cropped short and stuck out stiffly from her head. Her round, rosy cheeks were like those of a chipmunk stuffed full with pine nuts. Although the girl's face and hands were dusty and dirty, her dark eyes sparkled as she looked up shyly at Eliza.

She pointed to Eliza and said, "Miss Healy." Then she pointed to herself and said, "Taku."

"Thank you, Taku," Eliza said. "How did you learn some English?"

"My brother go Bishop House School, three years," Taku told her, holding up three fingers. "He want teach me what know."

"I will need your help, I think," Eliza said as she pointed to herself again. "Miss Healy." She wrote her name on the black portion of the wall. Then she pointed at Taku, said her name, and wrote it on the wall. She pointed to the next girl and said, "What is your name?"

"Kikshaw," said the girl as Eliza wrote it on the black wall.

As the other girls said their names, Eliza wrote them on the black wall also: Enola, Sutu'ya, Miwok, Saka, Minuk, Ka'sasee.

When a girl made a popping sound as she finished pronouncing her name, Eliza noted the place with an apostrophe as she wrote it on the black wall.

Eliza handed out the slates—small rectangles of shale with wooden frames along the sides to cover the sharp edges—and a small piece of chalk. She then wrote her name over and over on the black wall to model what she wanted the girls to do. She pointed to a name and then pointed to that girl. The girls tried to write their names several times. Eliza walked behind the girls as they worked, helping them when needed. Eliza could see that these girls had never written before. She recognized that she had a big job ahead of her.

As Eliza walked around the room, she wondered what she could teach next. Not knowing what else to do, Eliza pointed at different features in the room and said the objects' names, indicating that the girls should repeat the words. She pointed to the table, the chair, the window, and the benches. Then she realized there were no tables, benches, or chairs in a Tlingit home.

Eliza decided to teach something more personal, such as body parts. Pointing to her hair and then Taku's hair, Eliza said, "Hair."

The girls giggled and acted shyly as she used their hands, noses, and eyes as examples and motioned for them to repeat the words after her. Then she extended what she had taught them by saying

"This is my nose" and "This is your nose." Eliza continued teaching these phrases.

The Russian teacher of the older girls came to tell the class that it was lunchtime. The girls stood up and walked in line to the classroom for the older girls. As soon as they reached the door, they ran to get their lunches: a thin root-vegetable soup and dark Russian bread from some women in Russian dress. They ate their lunches, and then they ran to play in the yard in front of the school.

Eliza grabbed the lunch she had brought. She had a slice of bread and a potato cooked in the coals of the Healys' cook fire. She went outside to look for Katrina and Erm. When she spotted her friends, she was surprised to see that Max, Katrina's brother, was with them. The tall, handsome Tlingit and the young miner who had shown her and Katrina home the week before stood with them.

CHAPTER 16

K atrina greeted Eliza, saying, "Come join us. Do you know everyone?"

"I don't think you know Monutat," Erm interrupted, gesturing to the tall Tlingit warrior. "He is my friend. He come from village north of Sitka. He is from the Raven Clan, not Eagle."

"It is so nice to meet you," Eliza said.

The young miner stepped forward. "I don't think we were properly introduced the other week. My name is Jed."

"Hello, Jed. It's nice to see you again. Thank you so much for saving us from the forest. Do you come to school too?"

"Well, I come to school, but I'm teaching the younger boys. I hear you are now teaching the younger girls," Jed told her.

"You are? Maybe you can help me. I really have no idea what I'm doing. I must talk to you and see what you are doing. Have you taught before?" Eliza asked.

"Yes, this is my second year. Father Iakov drafted me last year. I know what you mean when you say you don't know where to begin," Jed said with a sympathetic smile. "I'll be glad to help you."

"Thank you. I have to go straight home after school today. Perhaps you could come over to help me to know what to do tomorrow," Eliza said, completely ignoring Max. He was casually leaning on the woodpile next to a small shed. He seemed to be ignoring her too.

"This afternoon, we will go to Saint Michael's Cathedral for our religion lesson, so you will not need to worry about teaching any more today," Jed said. "We go to the cathedral every Monday."

Eliza was relieved that she would not have to teach in the afternoon. She wanted to be prepared for the next class she taught. At the same time, she was excited about finally seeing the Russian Orthodox church, but she was concerned about what Father Iakov would teach.

As if reading Eliza's mind, Jed said, "Father Iakov reads scriptures and then does a service in Russian. I can only understand a little of what is being said. The music is in Russian too. There are cantors and singers to sing the songs."

"I think it will be very interesting. Katrina said there are pictures painted on the wall and beautiful icons of Jesus and the apostles," Eliza said as she sat down, leaning against the woodpile.

As they ate and talked, some chickens were scratching in the dirt. Several baby chicks scurried around behind their mothers. When Eliza put her hand out to the chickens, the babies darted under their mothers' wings. The hens clucked loudly and lowered themselves over their chicks.

Eliza laughed and said, "Did you know that God is like a mother hen?"

"What you mean?" Katrina asked.

"God is always ready to protect us, just like a mother hen is ready to protect her chicks. The chicks know they will be safe if they are under their mother's wings. The mother will protect them with her life. On the prairie, when we traveled to San Francisco, we saw where mother prairie hens covered their chicks through a prairie fire. When we lifted the charred bodies of the mothers, the chicks scurried out. The mother hens died so that their chicks could live. God is like that. He even gave His life so that we may live. And we can feel God's protection," Eliza said as she tried to catch a baby chick.

Eliza paused. Why hadn't God protected Amos? Did she really believe this anymore? God had protected them on their trip to Sitka.

Now had God abandoned them, or was it Satan attacking them because they were doing God's work? Satan didn't like that.

Katrina came to sit beside her while Erm sat cross-legged opposite them.

"God not die. He in heaven with Mary, Jesus, and the saints," Katrina said. "We see the picture on the ceiling of the cathedral."

"Who do you think Jesus is?" Eliza asked. "Was He a good teacher, just a man, or the Son of God?"

"Mary is Jesus's mother. She is blessed," Katrina said.

"Yes, you are right, but who is Jesus? In the Bible, Jesus said that He is God's own Son. Do you believe that?" Eliza asked.

"I have not read Bible. Father Iakov say, Jesus is Mary's son. God sent Him to die on cross," Katrina said. "If we believe in God, we do many good things. We help others and obey our parents and the church laws."

"Do you have just one God?" asked Erm.

"Yes, we have one God, but He is three persons. This is hard to understand. There is God the Father, God the Son—called Jesus—and God the Holy Spirit. God has been here since before the world began. God created everything that is in the earth, the water, the trees, the animals," Eliza tried to explain.

"We have spirits too," said Erm. "Everything has a spirit, the trees, the bear, the salmon. Yehl is the great spirit and creator. He created himself and then world. He turn two grass into Tlingit man and woman," she continued, picking up two blades of grass. "The Tlingit grew many. Go far and wide. Then dark covered the sky. All life stop. A Tlingit took sun and hide in box. Raven find box. He take sun high in sky. After many years, a great flood come. All died but two Tlingit. Raven put them on mountain. The water dry up. One went down in earth. He hold earth up from water. Other is Great Thunderbird, Hahtla. His wings make thunder. Eyes make lightning. Raven give them strong spirits. Raven give spirits to all."

"Erm, so much of your story is like the stories in the Bible. God is the creator, but He did not create Himself. Then He could not be God. He would just be a created being like us," Eliza responded. "God has always existed. God the Father, God the Son, and God the Holy Spirit created everything you see. We have a story about a flood in the Bible too. God sent the flood to rid the earth of all of the sinful people. He saved a man named Noah and his family on a large boat that Noah built. God told him to bring a male and female of every animal on the earth to put in the boat they called the ark. It rained for forty days and forty nights. As the waters dried up, the boat landed on a mountain, and Noah's family and the animals went and spread over the whole earth."

"Maybe history is same. We tell the stories in different ways," said Katrina.

"Yes, many religions have a creation and a flood story. I think that these were real events that all people know and pass down through their cultures. But it is important that we know the true story," Eliza said.

"But how we know which story to believe?" Katrina asked.

Eliza felt one of the pins in her hair fall out. As she looked for it, she said, "That is what makes it so difficult. It would be great if we all believed the same. Then perhaps we would all know."

Eliza's braids began to come loose from her head. All of the pins were falling out of her hair. Finally, her braids fell to her back. She stood up and looked for her hairpins, but she couldn't find a single one. She sat down again. Then her braid seemed to be alive, pulling her head back to the side of the woodpile.

"Ouch!" she exclaimed. "What is happening?"

Katrina began to giggle, and Erm covered her smile behind her hands.

As Eliza pulled her head and hopefully her braid from the woodpile, her head flew forward, and she landed head first in the dirt at Erm's feet. Then she heard loud, roaring laughter.

When Eliza got up she turned to look, there stood Max behind the woodpile with her hairpins in his hand.

"Remember I say Max give me headaches?" Katrina laughed. "You must have headache now."

Eliza's face turned bright red. She held her head where her braid had been pulled. For the first time in her life, she did not know what to say.

"Here your hairpins," Max said with a smirk. "I like your yellow hair. It look like shining gold when sun shine on it."

Eliza turned her back and pinned up her hair. She turned and glared at Max again. "Don't ever do that again!"

Just then, Father Iakov rang the school bell. All of the children lined up to walk to the cathedral three streets away. As the children made the slight left turn up the newly named Lincoln Street, the cathedral came into view.

CHAPTER 17

It was not a tall building but was made from wooden logs planed smooth on the outside. Two domes rose above the roof, a large one and a small one. They were not round but shaped like onions. There were bells in each of the domes. As they rounded to the front of the building, Eliza realized that the cathedral sat in the middle of the street that went down to the wharf. She carefully climbed the four steps in the front and entered with Katrina and Erm. The boys followed behind. As they entered, Katrina took Eliza's hand and pulled her to the left side of the sanctuary. The boys moved to the right. There were no chairs. All of the children were standing silently.

Eliza looked around the large room. There was a painting that filled the ceiling inside the larger dome. Around the outside walls were beautiful icons lined with silver. In the front, behind where Father Iakov stood, was a wall painted with pictures of Joseph, Mary, and Jesus. On both sides of the center picture, other people were painted, seven on each side. Gold leaf caused each figure to shine in the afternoon sun that beamed in the windows. Eliza could tell that twelve of the figures were Jesus's disciples, but the other two she did not know. One figure was in colorful priestly robes, while the other was dressed similarly to other Russians and held a replica of the cathedral in his hands.

Father Iakov started the service by singing a chant, which the cantor and choir answered with their own song. Father Iakov continued with the service, singing, reading from the Bible, and praying in Russian.

Eliza shifted uneasily on her feet. It felt as if she had been standing there for days, but it had only been two hours. The younger children were beginning to fidget but had remained quiet most of the time. She wished she could sit on the bench in the back, but it was filled with older women.

Father Iakov disappeared through an ornate door in the middle of the wall behind him. The choir sang a song. When Father Iakov returned, he raised a golden plate of bread above his head and then a large golden goblet as he and the choir sang. When he brought them forward, the nuns from the school guided the Russian children and some of the Tlingit children to the front. Each was given a bit of bread and drank from the cup. Some stepped back and knelt down and seemed to be praying.

Finally, the service was over, and the children filed out of the church. Eliza turned to Katrina and asked, "Do you think Father Iakov would talk to me about the Russian Orthodox Church?"

"I will ask him. I am sure he will," Katrina said as she started walking toward the front where Father Iakov was clearing the altar with the help of the nuns.

"Father Iakov," Katrina said.

He turned to her and asked, "*Da*, Katrina. How can I help you?"

"Eliza would like to ask you some questions about the church. She has been telling me about her faith, and she wants to know about mine. I was not able to answer her questions well," Katrina said.

"Of course," Father Iakov said as he headed to where Eliza stood.

Monutat, Erm, Max, and Jed said their good-byes and left the church so that Eliza and Father Iakov could talk.

"Well, I hear you did very vell this morning teaching the children. I am so glad you are able to teach them. Thank you. Vat questions do you have about the church?" he asked.

"I have many questions, but first, could you tell me about the pictures around this room?" Eliza asked.

"In the front, you see a picture of Jesus with Mary and Joseph on each side. The six men on each side are the disciples, twelve in all. The man on this side vith the beautiful robes is Bishop Innocent. He vas the first Russian bishop to come to build a church in Alaska. This church vas built in 1848. He vent back to Russia and is now the patriarch of the whole church in Russia. On the other side of icon, Governor Baranov is holding a replica of the church, because he gave the money so this church might be built. Ve honor him for his generosity, vhich is highly valued in our church. He returned to Russia vhen his vife, Maria, died. Her grave is a place of honor because her husband gave the money to build the church.

"The other pictures and icons are other saints of the Orthodox Church, and the special one in front is of Mary, the mother of Jesus. Many people come to pray to her, because she is the Mother of God and can speak to her son, Jesus, for the people," Father Iakov continued. "If you kiss her icon, she vill bring you good luck."

Without thinking, Eliza said, "We don't need to pray to Mary. We can pray right to Jesus. He tells God about our needs and confessions. It says in the Bible that Jesus is our mediator and advocate to the Father." Eliza covered her mouth. She could not believe she had just argued with Father Iakov.

"People are afraid to go directly to Jesus, and God is too holy for us to talk to Him," Father Iakov replied. "It is more comfortable for the Tlingit to pray to Mary or the other saints. They feel as if the saints are like the spirits in their religion. The church must meet the people vere they are and vith vat they can understand."

"Yes, we believe that too. My father is trying to learn as much about the Tlingit as he can so that he can teach them lessons they will understand," said Eliza. "Thank you for telling me about what you believe. Maybe we can talk again later. I need to go to the general store to mail a letter to my grandmother. My mother needs me at home soon."

"Good-bye. Until tomorrow," Father Iakov said.

Erm had waited outside the cathedral for Eliza and Katrina, and they headed down the street to the general store. As they went in the door, Max jumped out from behind a rain barrel as they passed. The girls ignored him, but he joined them anyway.

Eliza turned away from him and headed to the counter to buy her stamps. In the back of the store, there were several gold miners looking at picks and shovels. The miners glanced at them and began talking loudly.

Katrina whispered to Eliza, "The gold miners think we don't understand what they are saying. They say mean things about Russians and the Tlingit."

Erm had gone to the side of the store near the miners to look at bolts of cloth for her mother. Suddenly, one of the miners reached out and grabbed her arm.

"Look what we have here. A squaw girl," he said, jerking her from where she had stood.

Eliza immediately paid for her stamps and left her letter on the counter.

"Leave her alone! She is not bothering you!" she yelled, running into the man.

"All the Tlingit bother me! They're savages!" he yelled.

One of the other men grabbed Eliza as she pounded him with her fists. She could not keep her balance, and the man lifted her off the floor.

All of a sudden, the third man went flying as Max ran full force into him. The other men released the girls in their delight to have a fight with a Russian. Soon, all three men were trying to get their hands on Max.

"Get out of my store!" yelled Mr. Guillard, the storekeeper, "or I will hang you all out to dry!"

The fight moved toward the front of the store. Eliza, Katrina, and Erm backed out of the door just as the men threw Max into the street. Suddenly, there was another man in the fight with Max. The odds were more even now. All Eliza could distinguish were flying fists and wild black and red hair.

CHAPTER 18

Mr. Guillard and Ben, the big gold miner, stepped in and broke up the fight.

"You jerks get back to your slimy tents, and leave these young folks alone. You should be ashamed of yourselves," Ben said, dusting off his hat.

Max and the other young man stood up, attempting to brush the mud from their clothes. Eliza was surprised to see Jed standing there covered in mud and with blood running from a cut over his eye. Max did not look much better.

"Are you all right?" asked Eliza.

"Yeah, sure," Jed said.

Max looked at Eliza as if to ask if she were concerned about him too.

Eliza turned on her heel and put her nose in the air. "I have to get home right away. See you all tomorrow."

Jed ran to catch up with her. "Here, I will walk you home," he said.

Eliza slowed her step to match his. "Maybe you can tell me what to do with the children tomorrow."

Jed said, "Sure."

* * * *

When they reached Eliza's tent, her mother thrust Amos into Eliza's arms.

"Where have you been? I have been waiting and waiting for you. Now I am late to have tea with the other women and introduce them to the idea of having a Bible study. I must run, and you will need to fix dinner. Your father is meeting with some men who came to church last Sunday. Why can't you be where you are supposed to be?"

Eliza stood stunned. Yes, she was a bit late, but she was doing good things. She had taught the class, talked to her friends about God, learned more about the Russian Orthodox Church, and saved Erm from the gold miners. Her mother had not even wanted to hear what had happened to her today. Then she remembered Jed was standing there. She hid her face in Amos's hair and turned so that Jed could not see her red face.

"That was a bit rough, Eliza. Are you all right?" Jed asked quietly after her mother stormed away.

"Yes, I'm okay," Eliza said, her back still turned toward Jed.

"I'll tell you what," Jed said with a pretended jovial voice. "I'll play with Amos while you fix supper. I'd make you up some great flapjacks, but maybe not today."

Eliza realized what a help that would be as she began building up the fire and getting things from the larder to make supper. As she worked, she realized why her mother needed her so much, even for the regular chores of the day, not to mention all of the other things her mother was trying to do to help her father. With Amos so sick, her mother was not as free to take him along with her when she met with the women or helped with the church meetings. Simply having Jed entertain Amos made her work so much easier.

While she peeled potatoes, Eliza watched Jed playing with Amos. Jed was about a head taller than Eliza. His hair was the color of burnt-orange leaves in fall. His face and arms were covered with freckles, many more than the ones sprinkled across her nose. His eyes were a startling blue that matched the sea on a sunlit day. He was not that handsome. In fact, he looked a bit awkward with his long legs and long arms. But with his gentleness, quiet spirit, and helpfulness, he seemed very special to Eliza.

"What are you thinking about doing tomorrow for school?" Jed asked.

Eliza said, "I just wonder what else I should be doing besides reading, writing, and arithmetic. Even I am getting a little bored."

"I thought that last year too," Jed replied. "I wanted to make the learning to relate to their lives. The boys were learning to hunt and fish, so I had them share what they were learning in their villages. We talked and wrote about it. They loved sharing and worked hard on the projects we did."

"That's a great idea! The girls already want to tell me about the things they have made," Eliza said. "I'll plan some lessons around that. Thanks."

"What's going on here?" her father said sternly as he came around the corner of tent. Taking Eliza into the tent, he continued quietly. "This doesn't seem right for a young man to be here with you alone. Eliza, you are not a little girl anymore, and you must think of appearances."

"Father, that is Jed. He helped Katrina and me get home the other week. He is a teacher at the school too, and he was giving me ideas to teach the girls tomorrow. Mother had to go to the ladies' meeting and left me to care for Amos and cook supper. Jed offered to stay and watch Amos so I could cook." Eliza could not get the words out fast enough. She had been in so much trouble she did not need to do anything more to anger her parents. "We've just been talking."

When they emerged from the tent, Jed offered his hand and said, "Hello, Pastor Healy. We met last Sunday at the church meeting."

"Ah, yes, I remember you now. We had that nice chat after services. I did not recognize you at first," Mr. Healy said. "How is the mining going?"

"I'm not going to have much time to mine for a while. I'm teaching the younger boys at school. Father Iakov drafted Eliza to teach the younger girls today. It was quite a surprise for her," Jed responded.

Father threw back his head and gave a hearty laugh, and then he took Amos on his knee and bounced him up and down. Amos gave a weak smile.

"How did it go, Eliza?"

"Did you know Father Iakov was going to ask me to teach?" Eliza asked.

"I knew he wanted you to, but I did not think he would start you today." Father laughed. "So how did it go?"

"I was scared to death. I had no idea how to even start. I ended up teaching them 'hello' and their names. I wrote their names on the board, and then they spent the morning learning to write their names. There is one little girl that knows some English. If it weren't for Taku, I think it would have been a disaster. She is going to be my helper. Jed gave me some ideas for tomorrow. We will start with the alphabet and their sounds."

"Sounds like you will do a great job! What's for supper tonight?" he asked Eliza.

"Salmon. Mother bought two large ones this morning from the man who comes around to sell fish. We'll have boiled potatoes and bread too," Eliza answered.

"Is there enough to feed this strapping young man?" Father asked.

"There is plenty. I will throw an extra potato in the pot." A smile crept across Eliza face as she ducked her head into the tent to get another potato.

It was still daylight when Mother returned home. Dinner was ready, and they all sat down to eat. Mother told about how many ladies had come to tea. She described the Russian home where the tea was held.

"Did you know that every good Russian home has a piano?" Mother asked. "Even in Alaska. Oh, how I wish I could play the piano again. The air organ is all right, but a piano like Grandmother has would be so wonderful."

After dinner, Mother took Amos into the tent to change him and get him ready for bed. She gave him another dose of medicine and nursed him to sleep.

Eliza poured coffee for her father, Jed, and herself. Mother would get her own when she finished with Amos and had tucked him into bed.

"So what did you think of the service on Sunday?" Father asked Jed.

"It was great. I liked how you told everyone about the love of God. It is so important that people know how God first loved us. God sent his Son, Jesus, to save us from the things we do wrong. Sometimes we sin, and we don't even realize it. God will forgive us of all of our sins. God asks us to confess our sins, and He is faithful to forgive us. Wow, when I think of all of the things I've done wrong, I can't believe that God could forgive me," Jed said. "That was a great message."

"Are you a Christian?" asked Eliza, surprised.

"Yes, I have been a Christian since I was a child. After my parents died of cholera, I only had God to depend on. He has been so faithful in taking care of me. I miss the love of my parents, but I know that God loves me with an unconditional love," Jed said quietly.

"That's wonderful! I feel that way too. No matter what I do wrong, God is always ready and willing to forgive me. We only need to ask Him. It is so freeing to know I will not have to pay for my sins," Eliza continued. "People need to know this." Eliza then asked, "Father, what have you learned about the Orthodox and Tlingit faiths?"

"Well, the Orthodox certainly believe in God and the Trinity. They also revere Mary, because she was chosen to bear God's Son. We believe she was a woman of great faith, or God would not have chosen her for such a great task. But Mary is just a created being like us. She is not a divine being. There is no recorded information that tells us what Mary did after Christ's ascension. Some faiths have decided to make her almost as divine as God, an equal to Jesus. No one can be equal to God or Jesus. We must be careful about believing what men have added to the Word of God. Often, it is not what God intended and is often contrary to what the Bible teaches."

"Do you find them very generous as a result of their faith?" Jed asked.

"I know Katrina is very generous," said Eliza. "When I first came to Alaska in March, there were many cold, wet, and windy days here on the beach. She brought me a beautiful parka that will be just right when the snows come again."

"Yes, I have found that too. They have helped so much with building the benches and preparing for the Sunday meetings." Pouring himself another cup of coffee, Father added, "Father Iakov loaned us the air organ. As you know, Mrs. Healy was invited to one of the Russian officers' homes for tea today. She talked to the ladies about starting a women's Bible study. Friendships and relationships are very important to the Orthodox."

"And what about the Tlingit?" Eliza asked her father.

"Now that is a different story. The Tlingit are also generous. They really understand nature and can read the signs it gives. They just need to know these signs come from God, a natural part of His creation. Because of their reverence for nature, they do not waste a thing. They put back into the land whatever they cannot use. They may be fierce warriors when it comes to enemy tribes, but they are just defending their families, food sources, and hunting territories. God gives that responsibility to all men."

"What about all of the spirits they think are in the world, Mr. Healy?"

"That is something I am still looking into," Father said to Jed, but he looked at Eliza. "I have not had a chance to tell you. You will never guess who sat behind a tree while the meeting was going on Sunday."

"Who?" asked Eliza.

Jed said with a laugh, "The shaman!"

Chapter 19

Eliza went to school early each morning. Today, she carried her Bible and several rolled-up papers. Mr. Guillard, the French storekeeper, always wrapped purchases in brown paper, and Mother had saved every piece. Eliza had spent several nights making large signs for her classroom. She had made one for the alphabet with pictures of something that started with each letter, trying to use objects that the Tlingit girls would recognize. On another, she had written the numbers to ten and the words for each number. In a bag, she carried scraps of wood in straight and curved shapes, which her father had helped her make.

As she trudged up the beach, Jed came to meet her to walk to school. He had all his material in his knapsack.

"Can I help you carry something?" he asked.

"Yes, that would be nice," Eliza said as she handed him the rolls of paper.

"Looks like you've been busy," Jed said.

"After talking to you after school last week, I began to get all kinds of ideas that will help me teach the girls. Thank you so much. Once I think of one thing, another idea comes to mind. I find it's fun and exciting to come up with new ideas," Eliza said, excitement glowing in her eyes.

"I will have to start asking you for ideas soon," Jed said.

That morning, Eliza showed the girls the signs and the wooden pieces. She told the girls that they would need to work together using the wooden pieces. She showed them how an a was made with a short straight piece and a curved piece. A b was made with a long, straight piece and a curved piece. She showed them that it was important where each piece was placed. They could make both the capital and lowercase letters with the pieces of wood. The girls worked together making each letter and writing it on their slates. Eliza came around helping the girls when they needed it.

"It is fun, Miss Healy," Taku said. "We learn with games."

Each day, Eliza wrote a short scripture on the board to teach the girls to read. One morning, the girls worked on "The words of the Lord are pure words, like silver in a fire." The girls' families made things of silver, so they knew what happened to silver when it was heated. It separated from anything that was impure. The impurities were thrown away, because they had no worth.

"I'm having so much fun," Eliza told Katrina and Erm as they walked home. "I can't wait until next week."

"I heard the girls in your class at lunch," Erm said. "They said you are a very good teacher."

"That is so good to hear," Eliza said with a smile. "Father Iakov told me he had heard good reports too."

Jed ran up behind the girls. "Mind if I join you?"

"Oh, yes," said Katrina as she moved to walk beside him.

She walked a bit faster, and Jed moved along with her as he listened to her chatter away. They walked several feet in front of Eliza and Erm.

Katrina needed to go the other way, up Barracks Street to where her house was located. She ignored her turnoff and continued down to the tent city, talking to Jed.

Eliza walked with Erm but kept an eye on Jed and Katrina.

"I think Katrina likes Jed," Erm said.

Just then, Max came up behind Eliza and pulled on her apron strings until they came loose.

"Can you please stay away from me?" Eliza said, swatting at Max's hand so that he would let go of her ties.

"What do you think, Erm?" Max said. "I think Eliza likes me."

"No, I do not!" Eliza shouted. "I like Jed!"

When Eliza turned around, she saw that Katrina and Jed had stopped and were looking at her. Jed had a surprised smile on his face. Katrina's look was of surprised anger.

"I'd better get to my tent. I have a lot to do," Jed said as he turned at the first row of tents.

Katrina stormed over to Eliza. "Max likes you. You should be paying more attention to him," she fussed. "Jed is eighteen. He is much too old for you. Max is sixteen. He is much more suited to you."

Not wanting to hurt Max or Katrina, Eliza said, "I am much too young to be courted by either of them."

"No, you not too young," said Erm. "I have news for you. I tell you now. My aunt agreed. I marry Monutat. I only thirteen summers. I get married."

Eliza had noticed that Monutat and Erm seemed to stand aside when the others had lunch. They always talked intently to one another. Erm had a sweet smile on her face, and she seemed to beam whenever she talked to Monutat.

"When?" asked Eliza with shock. "Surely your father will want you to wait until you are older."

"We wait for a while," Erm said. "But I don't think it will be long."

"Then I am old enough to marry Jed," said Katrina.

Eliza didn't know what to say. The thought troubled her for some reason. She felt jealous, but she only felt like she and Jed were friends. All she could do was change the subject. "Will you come to our Sunday meeting this week?"

"Will Jed be there?" Katrina asked.

Eliza answered quietly, "Yes."

"Then I am coming on Sunday," Katrina said with a smug look. "Come on, Max. We need to get home."

Eliza turned to Erm. "Do you think you can come?"

"I will ask my family. I will come if they say yes."

On Sunday, Eliza's parents went early to the clearing where they held their meetings. Eliza put on her best calico dress and a clean apron. Her dress was green with little pink flowers. She looked as if she floated on a flower-filled meadow. Then she dressed Amos warmly. She picked him up and started for the meeting.

CHAPTER 20

W hen she arrived at the clearing, all of the benches had been set up. Jed and her father were carrying the air organ from the bishop's house. People were milling around or finding a place on a bench. Eliza noticed that many of the people were the miners and the people who had been on the ship. She settled on the back bench with Amos and waited for the service to start.

Eliza noticed Katrina and Max come into the clearing. Katrina saw Eliza, but she led Max to another bench on the opposite side. Eliza realized that Katrina must still be angry with her. She didn't blame her, but she didn't know what to do. Eliza looked around for Erm, but she was not there.

The service began with the singing of familiar hymns. Her mother played the organ, and her father led the people with his strong tenor voice. Amos made little bounces and swayed his head while the people sang. Eliza sang the songs, smiling as Amos danced in her arms. Then he started coughing. Eliza put him to her shoulder and patted his back until he stopped. He then curled up in Eliza's arms and started to suck his thumb, worn out.

"Welcome to our service this morning," her father said. "Today we will read from the book of Romans. 'For all have sinned and fall short of the glory of God.' The Ten Commandments are the laws of God. There is no one who has not broken one of the Ten Commandments. Have you ever lied? Have you ever taken something that does not belong to you or you wished you had what another person had? Did you always obey and honor your parents? I hear the Lord's name taken in vain many times a day. If you have done any of these things, then you have sinned. It is like a chain. You break one link, and the whole chain is broken."

Eliza observed a movement from the edge of the forest. Erm walked into the clearing. Eliza sat up and made a small wave to attract Erm's attention. Erm saw her and quickly came to sit on the bench beside her.

Her father went on. "'For the wages of sin is death, but the gift of God is eternal life in Christ Jesus, Our Lord.' Our sin separates us from God. Not only will we experience a physical death, but those who do not believe will also experience spiritual death."

Eliza glanced over at Katrina and Max. Katrina was staring at Jed, who was sitting on the bench in front of her. He must have arrived while they were singing. Troubled, Eliza looked away.

"'God demonstrates His own love for us, in that while we were yet sinners Christ died for us.' Because God loves us so, He sent His Son, Jesus, to pay the price for our sins. It is God's love that saves us, not a religion or a church."

Amos laid his head on Eliza's shoulder and put his thumb in his mouth. Soon, he was fast asleep. Eliza shifted his weight on her arm.

When Eliza glanced at Erm, she appeared to be listening carefully to what Mr. Healy was saying.

"'Whoever will call on the name of Jesus will be saved. If you confess with your mouth that Jesus is Lord, and believe in your heart that God raised Jesus from the dead, you shall be saved; for with the heart man believes, resulting in righteousness, and with the mouth confesses, resulting in salvation.' Confess your sins to God. Believe that Jesus's sacrifice on the cross has covered those sins. It takes faith in God and His plan for you to believe."

Some of the miners shifted on their benches. One miner stood up and said, "I still don't understand how God does what you said. I know I've sinned. Many times. I don't think God can forgive me like that."

"Are you married? Do you have children?" asked her father.

"Yeah, they are still down south," the miner replied.

"Would you do anything to protect them from harm?" her father went on.

"Yeah, we had some outlaws attack our wagon on our way out to Oregon. I jumped on one. I would have done anything that was needed to protect my family. I near got killed that day," the miner said.

"You did that because you love them, right?" her father asked.

"Yup, I would have fought them 'til they killed me," answered the miner.

"God loves you so much He was willing to come down to the world to die for you so that you or anyone can be saved."

The miner looked down at the ground for a moment. "I know I love my family. If God loves me even more than I love them, then He must love us mightily." He slowly sat down again.

"That's right," her father said. "God wants all of us to believe in Him and be saved. He wants our spiritual life to live with Him forever."

"Our last scripture today is taken from the book of Revelation. 'Behold, I stand at the door and knock, if anyone hears My voice and opens the door, I will come in to him.' Is God knocking at the door of your heart? Will you ask Him to come in? Is there anyone who would like to ask Jesus to come into his heart and life? If you feel Him knocking and would like to pray to receive Him, come up front, and I will pray with you."

After the end of the service, Eliza's father prayed with a few of the miners who had come to the front. Eliza noticed another movement at the edge of the clearing. A Tlingit stepped out from behind a large tree. He wore a brightly decorated blanket over his shoulders. Eliza recognized the blanket and the stature of the man. She gasped.

"Erm, who is that person coming out of the forest over there?" Eliza asked, shaking. "Is it who I think it is?"

"If you think he shaman, you are right," Erm said.

"What is he doing here? Do you think he will make trouble?" asked Eliza.

"I don't know why he is here. He will not harm us here with all these men," Erm said.

The shaman remained at the edge of the clearing.

"He's looking at my father. Do you think the shaman has come to hurt my father because he is teaching a different religion?" asked Eliza.

"There are only a few Tlingit here today. I don't think it is enough to bother the shaman," Erm said.

Eliza's father was talking to the miners who had come to the front. Several other miners had wandered up front and were talking to him too. Suddenly, he looked up and saw the shaman. Her father politely excused himself and began walking toward the shaman.

"Oh no! What is he doing?" gasped Eliza, putting her hand over her mouth, her eyes wide.

The shaman and her father talked for a moment, and then the shaman handed a small bag to her father. Her father nodded and tipped his hat. The shaman bent slightly at the waist and backed into the forest again.

Eliza's mother came to stand by Eliza and Erm. As Eliza's father walked toward them, Eliza handed the sleeping Amos to her mother and ran to her father.

"What did you talk to the shaman about? What did he give you? Aren't you afraid of him?" Eliza asked.

"There is no need to be afraid of him. He is a very nice, intelligent man. He has come to the clearing every day since our first Sunday meeting. We have talked many times. He went to school in Juneau and learned a bit of English," her father said.

"But, Father, what did he give you?" Eliza asked.

"It is a combination of certain plants and roots. The shaman said we should make a strong tea out of it and give it to Amos. He said it would make him well," her father answered. "I am willing to try anything. I have not given up on God; God has created things that we can use to heal us."

CHAPTER 21

The warm August sun beat down on the white tents on the shore of Sitka Bay. Eliza lugged two buckets of water from Swan Lake near the cathedral down the hill to their tent. She stopped to mop her brow. She didn't know how Mother had done this each week to do the laundry. This was hard, heavy work. A pang of guilt ran through her heart as she realized how little she had done to help her mother.

Mother planned to do the washing each Saturday so that Eliza could help. There really wasn't that much laundry to do since each member of the family didn't have but two or three changes of clothing. The biggest load was always the white cloths they used for diapers, and her mother needed to wash them almost every day. Eliza wished her mother would do as the Tlingit mothers, who let their children under two go naked from the waist down. *It sure would save all those trips up and down the hill to Swan Lake*, she thought. Eliza smiled to herself as she remembered the sight at the village. She couldn't imagine letting Amos do that. She picked up the buckets again and trudged down the hill.

As Eliza hung the wet clothes on a line strung between their tent and the next, Jed came by. Eliza immediately went to tell her mother that Jed was there. Her father had told her to be sure someone was with her when Jed was around so that no one would think she was not behaving properly.

Removing his hat, Jed said, "Good morning, Mrs. Healy."

Mother returned the greeting and then asked, "Are you looking for Mr. Healy? He is up at the clearing, meeting with some of the miners."

"No, actually, I came by to see if Eliza would like to go for an outing this afternoon," he replied.

"You certainly cannot go by yourselves. You will need to ask Mr. Healy. Who can go with you to chaperone?" she asked.

"Eliza and Max have been asking about how to mine gold. I thought we could pack a picnic lunch and go to my claim up the river from Erm's village," Jed told her.

"Oh, pshaw, I don't think Eliza should go. It is too far and dangerous. It would be hard for a girl to climb up there," Mrs. Healy said, all aflutter. "Would just you and Max be going? Oh my, that is even worse."

"No, ma'am," assured Jed. "Max and his sister, Katrina, will be going. We will stop by the village to see if Erm and maybe Monutat can go."

Eliza's heart had been beating excitedly, but now it felt like it stopped altogether. Katrina had not spoken to her for almost four weeks. Yet if Katrina didn't go, there was no possibility that her father would let her go. Eliza thought it might not even be a good idea to go. Katrina would think Jed was asking her to go, not Eliza. She would be thrown at Max all afternoon. Now the trip didn't feel like it would be such an adventure, after all.

"Go ask Mr. Healy what he thinks," Mrs. Healy said with her arms crossed. Then she nervously brushed her hair off her forehead.

Eliza watched Jed walk away. What did his asking her to go mean?

"Mother, I will continue to help you with the rest of the wash," Eliza said. "I don't want to leave this all to you, even if Father says I can go."

Eliza hung up the last diaper and threw out the wash water. Just as she finished, Jed returned with Max and Katrina.

Eliza smiled at them and said, "Hi. It's good to see you."

Katrina looked away, but Max said hello in a gruff voice. He looked down and scuffed the dirt with his foot.

Soon Jed returned. "I picked up Max and Katrina on my way back from talking to Pastor Healy. He said that Eliza could go," Jed said. "I hope this arrangement meets with your approval."

Mother looked from one young person to another and then back again. "I am not sure I do approve, but if Mr. Healy said it was all right with him, I guess you may go."

As Jed picked up Amos, he asked, "How is Amos doing? He seems to have much better color and a bit of pep."

"He is doing much better. He has been taking the Tlingit tea for four weeks now," Mother said.

Max asked, "Did you ever find out what is in that tea?"

"Several plants and roots. The shaman said he used devil's club, *shaach*, a plant that grows in the swamp, crab apple tree bark, and the outer bark of fir, the kind that has pitch on it. It also contains elderberry and red alder root. He also gave us some eulachon fish oil to rub on his chest and to take a spoonful three times a day," Mother informed them. "Amos gets better each day. His cough is almost gone."

"That's wonderful, Mrs. Healy," Jed said.

As Eliza's mother went into the tent to give Amos another dose of Tlingit tea and put him down for a nap, Eliza glanced at Katrina. Katrina only had eyes for Jed and didn't say a word to her. Eliza wondered how this day would be if Katrina wasn't even going to talk to her. Maybe this wasn't such a good idea, after all.

"We need to pick up some supplies and my mining equipment. Then we will head out for Erm's village," Jeb told them.

As they walked along the trail to the village, Katrina walked with Jed. Max, carrying some supplies, fell in beside Eliza.

Wanting to at least be polite to Max, Eliza asked, "Can I help you carry anything?"

"No, I have everything," Max said. "I can even carry you."

"Oh no, you won't! By the way, does your family know what they are going to do when the territory is handed over to the United States in October?" Eliza asked, changing the subject.

"My father and mother go back to Russia. My father serve in the army there. I not know what I do yet. I want to stay and trap furs. There big market for them here and in Russia and America. I make big money," Max said. "My father want me come with them to Russia to join the military, but I want stay here."

"What about Katrina?" Eliza asked, almost tripping on a root in the path.

As Max steadied her and then pretended to let her fall, he said, "Who know? As you see, Katrina think Jed so wonderful. I think she like to stay and marry him. I not know why she think he marry her. He no pay any attention. She run to him when she see him."

Eliza watched Katrina and Jed as they walked several feet in front of them. Jed held his supply pack between them instead of on his back. He nodded politely as Katrina prattled on and on. Jed glanced back over his shoulder at Eliza a couple of times, giving her a sheepish grin.

"What about you?" Max asked. "What will you do when all the Russians leave?"

"My father is trying to bargain for one of the houses the Russians are leaving behind. We don't know which one we will get. There is a lottery, and we will be offered a house or two based on the number in our family. It will be good to finally have a house, no matter which one it is," Eliza said.

"I would give you our house if my father would let me," Max said. "I will just need a trapper's hut up in the mountains. I guess I would need to have a nicer place if I get married." Max looked at Eliza with raised eyebrows.

Eliza ignored Max's insinuation.

As they neared the clearing where Erm's village stood, Jed dropped back to walk with Max. Katrina did not have any choice but to walk with Eliza.

"Hello," Katrina said with a smirk. "I did not know you would be coming today."

"Why wouldn't I be coming? We are all friends, aren't we?" Eliza said defensively. "Friends always do things together. But I've missed seeing you at lunchtime at school."

"I want you to know that you cannot be good friends with Jed. He is my beau now," Katrina snapped.

"I think that is up to Jed. Did he say he was courting you?" Eliza asked.

"No, but you see how he always walk with me," Katrina said.

"Max tells me your family is going back to Russia. You will have to go with them too, won't you?" Eliza asked hopefully.

"I think Jed will ask me to stay and marry him," Katrina said.

"You really think so? After all, there are only two more months, so I guess he'd better hurry up and ask your father for your hand," Eliza said as she shrugged her shoulders and looked away.

"He will," Katrina said as they entered the village.

They found Erm sitting in the doorway of the Wolf House. Her face was downcast.

"Are you all right?" asked Eliza.

"I not feel good," Erm said as she rubbed her stomach.

"We are going up to my mining camp and hoped you might come with us," Jed said.

"I am waiting for Monutat. He will be here any time now," Erm said. "We were going to walk upriver anyway to pick elderberries. So maybe we go with you. I am so glad to see you both, Eliza and Katrina. I have missed our times together as friends."

"Yes, but I have told Eliza my plans with Jed, so I guess we can be friends again," Katrina said as she gave Eliza a meaningful look.

Eliza started to say something and then decided it didn't matter what would happen. It was all in God's hands anyway. Maybe Jed wasn't the man God had planned for her, but if he were the one, God would work things out. She wanted to be in God's will, and He would show her the way. She knew this was how God worked, but it was hard to wait on God sometimes or to know what His plans were for her. But Eliza knew a marriage wouldn't work if it wasn't in God's plan.

Just then, Monutat came out of the forest and joined them. "What we doing?" he asked.

CHAPTER 22

"I promised to take Max and Eliza up to my mining camp today and thought we would ask you whether you wanted to come along," said Jed. "I've brought supplies for a picnic."

"We will go with you," said Monutat. "We pick berries on the way back."

Erm slowly got up and went into the Wolf House. She returned with two beautifully woven reed baskets. Each had rows and designs woven into them with pine needles, which were dark against the light reeds.

Monutat and Erm started out with Jed gently guiding Eliza by her elbow. Katrina stood with her hands on her hips until Max said, "Come on. Let us just go."

Once they got beyond the Tlingit village, the trail became no more than a footpath. They followed the river but often had to climb over fallen trees and push bushes aside. The branches pulled at Eliza's and Katrina's skirts. Erm sat down on a fallen log, bending over as if in pain.

"Are you all right, Erm?" Eliza asked, putting her hand on Erm's shoulder.

"I okay," Erm said. "It only hurt sometime. I think I know what wrong. I tell you later."

Eliza took the opportunity to pull her skirt up from the back and tuck it into her waistband in front. This pulled her skirt in, and she appeared to have ballooning pantaloons on.

Katrina stood wide-eyed. "You look like you are wearing pants," she said.

"I am tired of the branches pulling at my skirt. I don't want it to get torn. This way I can climb over the trees much easier," Eliza said.

"It does not look very ladylike, does it, Jed?" Katrina asked, batting her eyes at him.

"Much more practical. That's a good idea, Eliza. Maybe you should try it," Jed said.

"Humph," Katrina said. "Come on, Max. Let us go."

"Let me lead the way from here. Come on, Eliza," Jed said.

Erm slowly stood up. Monutat took her arm. "Are you all right?" he asked again.

"I will be fine," Erm answered as she followed the others up the trail.

About another mile up the river, Eliza saw a small hut sitting next to the river. Washbasins, hacksaws, pails, and other equipment hung on the trees around the clearing. About twenty feet in front of the hut was a large hole in the ground with three sturdy branches tied together to make a tripod over it. A rope holding a dented bucket went through a pulley fastened at the peak of the tripod. The other end of the rope was tied to the trunk of a small tree. Mining pans hung on the walls of the hut.

"Well, this is it," said Jed. "Not much to look at, but I've gotten about ten dollars' worth of gold from this site in the last two years. With that and what Father Iakov pays me, I make out all right. But I have little to spare."

Eliza looked out over the sparkling waters of Indian River.

Jed's camp was about fifty yards from a magnificent waterfall. It was full since the snowcaps and glacier were melting from the summer sun. The water cascaded over the falls, roaring and rippling as it made its way over the large rocks tossed across the river bottom. There were a few salmon already swimming up the river to lay their eggs in the waters of a lake farther up.

Eliza turned to Jed and said, "This is so beautiful. The imposing mountains, the white of the snowcaps, the green of the trees, the sparkling blue water all thrown together is just majestic. I love the wildness of this country. I'm surprised you don't live up here all of the time."

"I might build a sturdier cabin up here for the late spring, summer, and fall, but it is too cold and dangerous up here in the winter. In the winter, there is always the chance of avalanches or large chunks of ice falling from the glacier and floating downstream. The icebergs push the water ahead of them, and when they crash over the waterfall, this whole area is flooded as the water comes up over the banks," Jed said.

"Yes, that happen to our village downstream. We must move away from the river during early melting time," Erm said. "That when we go north to our fish camp to net the eulachon fish for its oil. Eulachon oil very important to village for medicine, preserving food, and other things."

"That one advantage for Raven village. It built on edge of channel," said Monutat. "We build permanent homes on ridge above the sea."

"Who's hungry?" asked Jed. "Monutat and Max, do you think we can catch some salmon? I'll challenge you to catch some with your hands!"

"I do it all the time," Monutat said.

"I bet I can too," Max boasted.

"If we work together, we can have lunch in no time. Katrina and Eliza, there are potatoes in the knapsack. Would you mind peeling and slicing them for some fried potatoes? Erm, would you mind laying the fire there in that fire ring?" Jed asked, pointing to the fire pit surrounded by flat rocks with a couple of logs nearby to sit on.

Eliza grabbed a washbasin and went to the river to get water to wash the potatoes. When Eliza returned to the logs by the pit, Erm asked her to help her gather some wood for the fire.

"Which would you rather do, Katrina, peel potatoes or gather wood?" Eliza asked.

Katrina looked around. "I help gather wood. That be easy with all the fallen logs," she said.

As Erm and Katrina gathered wood, Eliza made short work of peeling and slicing the potatoes. She could hear the boys whooping and hollering as they scooped up several large salmon with their hands. She laughed and ran to the river to get a better look. She thought this must be a perfect day, with the beautiful scenery and the romping, playful actions of Jed, Monutat, and Max. She felt at peace here in this place. She sighed and turned back to help with the fire.

Erm made the fire while the boys cleaned the salmon. Jed told Eliza that there were two skillets hanging on the wall inside the hut.

The hut was dark inside, since it didn't have any windows. The only light came from the small door. The only things in the hut were a bed made from sturdy branches attached to the back wall, a couple of shelves, and several pegs by the door. On the wall were two cast-iron skillets and a couple of cooking pots. Their bottoms were black from the fires they had been used over many times. Eliza quickly took the skillets and returned outside. She felt embarrassed and felt that she was invading Jed's private space.

As the rocks around the fire heated up, Eliza set the cast-iron skillets on them to heat up. Jed took some lard from a can in his knapsack and put a couple of spoonfuls in each pan. The smell of fried potatoes and salmon soon filled the air. They sat on the logs and filled their tin plates with the delicious food.

Max, Jed, and Monutat joked and slapped each other on the back, enjoying their salmon catching again. The girls watched and giggled at their antics.

"Is it hard to catch a salmon with your hands?" asked Eliza.

"Not if you know how to do it," Jed joked.

"Tlingit do it best," said Monutat, laughing. "Max, did you catch any? Tell the girls how many you catch."

Max turned red. "I never caught one. They swim right through hands. They very fast."

"If you are up here and hungry, you would learn quickly," Jed said. "Otherwise, I would have starved last year."

"Oh, that be terrible!" said Katrina.

"I not think Jed not live," said Erm. "He know Tlingit ways."

Eliza looked at Jed. He would survive or learn how, she was sure. Jed's many accomplishments made him all the more interesting.

* * * *

While the others cleaned up, Jed asked Katrina to come with him. As they strolled by the river a moment, Jed stopped and turned to Katrina.

"One reason I wanted you all to come is to see this place and its beauty, but I want to talk to you about something that has been bothering me for the last month," Jed said. "Katrina, I think you are a very nice girl, and I have enjoyed talking with you, but I must tell you straight out, I'm not going to ask your father to court you. You'll be going back to Siberia with your parents soon, and that's what is best for you. I bet you'll meet some handsome Russian prince who will sweep you up and take you off on his white horse to his castle."

Katrina looked stunned. The moment was tense. Katrina didn't know what to say. She spun around and went running back to the hut. She hid behind it and began to sob.

Erm went to look for her. When she saw her red face, Erm knew that something was wrong. Katrina did not say a word. She pulled her hankie from her pocket and wiped her face and eyes.

"What happen?" Erm ask.

Katrina began crying again. "Jed said he would not marry me."

Erm put her arm around her shoulders. "Come walk with me a bit."

CHAPTER 23

When Jed approached the fire pit, he brushed his arm across his eyes a few times. Eliza, Monutat, and Max sat quietly, wondering what had happened.

"Who would like to find some gold?" asked Jed to break the silence.

Max, Monutat, and Eliza all jumped up and followed Jed to get the gold pans hanging on the hut's sides. Jed led them down to the river and explained how to pan for gold.

"First, you scoop some sand and rocks from the bottom of the river. Be sure there is some water in your pan," Jed said as he scooped up a small amount of sand and gravel with about a half pan of water. "Slowly swirl the water in the pan around the edges of the pan. Let small amounts of water slowly escape over the edges. Continue to swirl it until the sand and larger stones are washed over the sides. Gold is the heaviest of all and will stay in the bottom of the pan when all of the sand and gravel is washed out. When the pan is about empty, you might see small flecks or gold nuggets in the bottom. Take them out carefully and put them in this small washbasin."

Eliza, Max, and Monutat watched closely as Jed demonstrated the moves as he talked. When Jed got to the bottom of his pan, he found several tiny flakes of gold.

"You need to look very closely, or you might miss the gold," said Eliza.

"True, but when you get several of these flakes, it will add up to something. Go ahead and try it," Jed said as he scooped up another pan of sand.

* * * *

While the others were panning for gold in the river, Katrina and Erm came back and sat on a log by the fire.

Erm finally broke the silence. "What do you think about what Jed just told you?"

"I cannot believe it. We have spent a lot of time at school and walking home or other places. Jed seems to always walk with me," Katrina said.

"Does he walk with you, or do you walk with him?" Erm wanted to know.

Katrina thought about that for a while. "I guess maybe I always walk with him. Maybe I talk more than he talks."

"I think that is true. I think Jed is—what you say?—a gentleman. He would not want to ignore you if you come to walk with him. He would pay attention to you or anyone else that walked with him. He talk to me many times too," Erm pointed out.

"But why did he have to tell me here?" Katrina asked. "He could have told me anytime."

"It is not good for a boy and a girl to be alone. I think Jed would want to do the right thing," Erm said. "He want to be honest with you. He knew you would need someone to talk to. I think that is a good thing."

"My hope is all gone. I want to stay in Alaska, but now I have no one to be with. I will have to go with my parents back to Siberia. This has been my home for ten years. I do not remember Siberia. I do not know anyone there," Katrina said. "All I remember is my grandmother and an uncle, and I do not remember much. It will be like going to a strange place again."

"I think Sitka will change very much when more Americans are here," Erm said. "This will seem like a strange place too."

Katrina clasped her hands around her knees and buried her head in her skirt as she sat on the log. She rocked back and forth for a minute. She raised her head and glanced out to where Jed was showing Eliza some gold in her pan.

Katrina jumped up. "You are right, Erm! My father knows many Russian noble families. I am sure they have sons just my age. I will find a handsome prince. My father will be sure I have a good match. There's no point in pining over Jed. I not want to live in a hut or tent."

"Oh, Katrina, that be so exciting to meet a prince. I can see it now," Erm said. "You will have a white fox parka with long fur around your beautiful face; your skirts blowing in wind as you throw kisses to your family. You ride off on your prince's white horse."

Katrina laughed. "Thank you for being my friend. But you sound too much like Jed."

"Eliza is your friend too. She misses you. Even if you like Jed, she was willing to let you be with him," Erm reminded her.

"*Da*, you are right. I thought she would want to take him away from me, but now I see he was never mine to take."

* * * *

Eliza and the boys came up from the river dripping wet and beaming.

"We found some gold! Look!" said Eliza as she showed Katrina and Erm the gold in the washbasin.

"There is not much there," Katrina commented.

"There is about fifty cents worth of gold in there," Jed said. "Some money today and some money next week adds up to enough."

"What is this big hole for?" asked Eliza, pointing to the hole with the tripod and bucket.

"Since there is some gold in the river, I thought there might be a vein of gold leading up to the river. This is the beginning of a gold mine," Jed said.

"How do you dig a mine?" asked Max.

"I need help when I look for gold in the hole. While someone holds the rope so I don't go down too fast, I ride down on the bucket with a pick axe and a shovel. As I dig more dirt out of the hole, I fill the bucket, and my partner pulls the bucket back up and pours the dirt into a pile on this slab of wood. When I have filled about four buckets, I sit on the bucket and my partner pulls me out of the hole. I help by putting my feet on the side and push myself up," Jed told them. "Ben helps me a lot, and some of the other miners help from time to time. I help them at their claims in return."

"Then what happens?" asked Eliza.

"I bring water up from the river and pan the dirt just like we pan for gold in the river," Jed said. "I can do that part on my own."

"Have you found any gold in the hole?" asked Max.

"No, so far I haven't found a vein of gold in the ground," Jed said. "If I do, I will need a sluice to wash out the dirt."

"What's a sluice?" asked Eliza.

"It's a long trough that has a floodgate on one end. You pour water down the trough over the dirt, and it washes the dirt away just like when we were panning for gold in the river. After the water is released little by little through the floodgate, gold stays in the sluice, and you can just pick it out," Jed explained.

Eliza was the only one who didn't look confused after Jed's long explanation. She could tell that Jed was excited by this work. Her excitement and curiosity were almost too much to bear.

"Anyone want to go down into the hole and dig some dirt?" Jed asked.

Max and Monutat volunteered to go down the hole. Eliza wanted to go too but knew it wouldn't really be proper for a girl.

Jed went down the hole to show the others how it was done. He came up after his first bucket with Monutat pulling the rope. Max went down next and also filled one bucket. Eliza took the bucket and poured it on the wooden slab. Next, Monutat went into the hole and filled a bucket.

As Monutat came out of the hole, Eliza asked, "Can I go down in the hole? Please let me try." She was on the verge of a little dance in anticipation.

"Are you sure?" Jed asked. "It's dirty and dark down there. The only light is the sunshine. The walls of the hole are a bit wet with water seeping in. You can see how muddy Max and Monutat are."

"That's all right. I would like to see what it's like. I'm very strong, and you boys will be able to pull me out on the bucket," Eliza said as she hiked her skirt up into her front waistband again.

Jed laughed. "You can try it if you want. Are you sure?"

"I may be a girl, but I can do this. I like to have new and exciting experiences. I think this might be the most dangerous one I have ever tried. But I would like to do it, if you don't mind."

Jed held the rope as Eliza carefully pulled the bucket to the side of the hole. She inched out over the edge of the hole until she could get her legs on the bucket and around the rope. She held the rope tightly. At first, the bucket swung out over the huge deep hole. Eliza had a very funny feeling in her stomach. *Please, God, keep me safe and be with me,* she prayed silently.

"I'm ready," she said as the bucket stopped swinging over the hole.

"All right. Here we go," Jed said as he began to lower Eliza into the hole.

Eliza descended into the semidarkness of the hole. The odor of wet soil filled her nostrils. She shivered in the cool air as she went farther from the warm sunlight. She felt like she was being lowered into her grave. The thought almost caused her to tell Jed to stop and pull her up again. *No, I started this, and I'll finish it,* Eliza decided.

"Let us just leave her down there!" Max shouted into the hole.

"You'd better not!" Eliza shouted as her feet touched the bottom of the hole. As she looked up the tunnel she had come through, it seemed much smaller. "How deep is this place, anyway?"

"I think it must be eighteen feet by now!" Jed shouted back.

The thought of being so deep underground made Eliza's skin crawl. She felt around for the shovel but couldn't find it. She moved around in the hole, peering through the dim light. As she turned, she fell back as her foot caught on the shovel as it lay on the ground.

Eliza screamed as she fell onto the damp earth at the bottom of the pit mine.

"Are you all right?" Jed shouted in a worried voice.

"Did you find the snakes down there?" Max shouted.

Another scream came from below. "I don't see any snakes down here. Just keep your thoughts to yourself!" Eliza shouted as she regained her composure. "I just tripped over the shovel. Tell Monutat to pick up after himself the next time."

Eliza picked up the shovel and began shoveling mud into the bucket. The handle on the shovel was wet and slimy. Eliza could taste the mud as the fumes rose from the fresh shovel cut.

"I think I made a big mistake," she mumbled as she dug her last bit of the mud. She could hear the others talking, and then she heard Jed's voice distinctly.

"That girl has a lot of spunk. I don't think anything would deter her from what she sets her mind to," he said. "I admire that in a girl."

Eliza felt a warm feeling as she listened. She soaked in Jed's comment for a moment. As she reflected on Jed's compliment, a warm pink glow rose up to her cheeks. She put her hands to her face and whispered, "Oh my, I can't believe I'm blushing."

Eliza pulled on the rope and shouted, "Haul up the bucket! It's full. Be sure you send it back down for me!"

"Don't worry. I won't let Max leave you there," Jed called as he pulled the bucket up.

As the bucket went up, Eliza felt more closed in than before. The bucket and rope were her lifeline to the world above. She knew

God was with her even down in this hole. It still seemed an eternity before she saw the bucket coming down again.

"Watch out below!" shouted Max. "We do not want to hit you."

The bucket came down slowly, and Eliza easily caught it with her hands and guided it to the bottom. She sat on the bucket but realized that her legs were not long enough to reach the side of the hole to help pull her weight up.

"My feet don't touch the walls," she informed those who held her life in their hands.

"Don't worry. There are three strong men to pull you up. I think we can handle that," Jed said.

"Not if I not help," said Max.

"Heave ho, boys," Jed said.

Eliza rose quickly with the three boys on the rope. Almost too fast. "Slow down a bit. If I were a kite, I would be in the sky at this rate."

As Eliza struggled out of the hole and onto solid ground, everyone was laughing. Katrina gasped and put her hands on her face, eyes wide.

"What did you do, take a mud bath down there?" Max teased.

Her dress, arms, and feet were covered with mud. "What am I going to do? My mother will be angry with me!" Eliza cried.

"You can go down to the river and wash up," Jed said with a big smile. "Just be sure you include your face."

"Oh my," Eliza said as she touched her face with her hands. "I must be a fright!"

"Now you can just say you are trying to make yourself more beautiful," Max said.

"What do you mean?" Eliza asked, wide-eyed.

"You have given yourself a nice mud pack on your face," Max said.

"Oh!" Eliza stormed off.

"Wait," said Jed. "Here is a towel. Don't take too long. It's getting late. It may stay light until ten o'clock, but I think your parents may want you home soon."

Eliza knew Jed was right. She didn't want her parents to be angry with her again.

When Eliza reached the river, she looked back toward the hut. Everyone was hidden behind it. She looked farther down the river and saw a large, thick clump of bushes along the edge. She made her way behind the bushes. She looked back up the shore and made a decision. She pulled her dress off over her head. She left her bloomers and chemise on and waded into the water. She washed out her dress and laid it on the bushes so she was hidden even more.

Eliza sat in a shallow pool and washed the mud off her body and face. She felt her hair and realized it was caked with mud too. Holding her nose she fell backward into the water, rinsing her hair with the other hand. She shivered from the cold water as she climbed out again, teeth chattering.

Katrina called out, "Eliza, are you all right? We heard a big splash. Did you fall in?"

"No, no!" Eliza called. "Don't come over here!"

Just as Eliza scrambled from the water, Katrina peered around the bushes and gasped.

CHAPTER 24

Eliza quickly grabbed the towel to hide her indiscreet attire. She toweled her hair and face. Her underthings were very wet, and her dress was still damp.

"Why did you do such a thing?" asked Katrina. "The boys are right over there."

"Where?" asked Eliza as she struggled into her wet dress. "Are they coming?"

"No, they are sitting on the logs on the other side of the house, talking while we wait for you," Katrina replied. "A decent girl would never do what you just did."

"Don't I look better now? I'm not as muddy. I may be wet, but the mud is gone. Everything should be dry by the time we get home. Besides, this is as private as when I take a bath in the tub in the tent. Although that water is much warmer," Eliza said as she pinned her long blonde braids around her head. "Please don't say anything to anybody! I didn't intend for anyone to see me. You have to promise that you won't tell anyone."

"I promise. I would not want a friend of mine to have people think bad of her," Katrina said as she smiled at Eliza and took her hand to lead her back to the others.

Eliza wasn't sure she could trust Katrina. She seemed friendly, but after the last few weeks, it seemed strange.

When they got back to the group, everyone was crowded around Jed. Eliza and Katrina joined them. Jed looked up and smiled at Eliza.

"We have divided the gold we found. Do you have a handkerchief, Eliza?" Jed asked.

"Yes, but it is a bit wet," Eliza replied as she held it out.

Jed poured a small amount of gold into it. "You should keep this. It is your gold. You worked hard for it. I gave each person a share. You should have some too," Jed said. "We'd better get going. Help me bring up some water, boys, to make sure the fire is out. We will help Monutat and Erm pick elderberries on the way down. We should be home in time for supper."

On the way back to Erm's village, the young people chatted about their exciting day. The girls soon had Erm's basket full. Monutat's did not fill as fast since the boys ate as many as they put in the basket.

When they got to Erm's village, Erm handed the baskets to her aunt. Her aunt spoke in Tlingit, but the smile on her face indicated that she was pleased. The girls gave Erm a hug, while the boys shook hands with Monutat.

"I'll see you at church tomorrow?" Eliza asked.

"Yes, Monutat is coming with me tomorrow," Erm told her.

"Wonderful. I will see you then," Eliza said. "Next week is the last week of school, and on Friday, the whole school is having a picnic. I think it will be fun to meet all of the Tlingit parents."

Eliza's clothes had nearly dried by the time they got back to the tent city. Neither her mother nor her father made any comment about her appearance.

Jed had escorted her home, spoke to Mr. Healy for a moment, and then waved good-bye, saying, "See you at church tomorrow."

At the Sunday meeting, Erm did not show up. Eliza watched for her most of the meeting, but neither Erm nor Monutat came. Eliza was sitting with Katrina, and Jed sat on the other side of the aisle with Max. Katrina helped entertain Amos until he got tired and curled up in Eliza's lap.

The shaman sat on a bench now instead of squatting in the forest. He had been coming each week and always came to say hello to Amos and to see how he was doing. There were more people coming each week. Several people had prayed to receive Christ into their lives. Ben, the big miner, was one of them, and he was trying hard not to drink so much. He had a kind heart and smiled much more. The miners had learned not to be so unruly and didn't interrupt the meetings now. So far, no Tlingit besides Erm and Monutat came to the meetings.

After the meeting was over, Eliza and her friends sat talking until the adults were ready to leave.

"I wonder why Erm didn't come today," commented Eliza.

"I noticed she didn't come too," Jed said. "I was watching for Monutat so I could invite him to sit with us."

"Maybe she not like long meetings," said Max with a grin.

"I guess we will find out tomorrow," Katrina added.

The next day, Erm did not come to school. She didn't come all week.

"I am worried about Erm," Eliza said at the picnic on Friday. It is not like her to be gone all week. She was not feeling well last Saturday. I hope it is not something serious."

"Me too," Katrina said. "I wonder if she just had work to do at the village."

"Her parents really want her to learn English. She has learned so much, but I think they would want her to continue to the end of school," Eliza reasoned.

"Maybe we can go to the village tomorrow and check on her. I'll ask my parents tonight, and you ask yours," Katrina said. "I will come by your tent if I can go."

Katrina arrived at Eliza's tent after lunch. Her parents had agreed to let Eliza go. They could see how worried Eliza was about Erm missing a whole week of school and not coming to church when Erm had said she was coming with Monutat.

As Eliza and Katrina walked to the Tlingit village, Katrina said, "I want to apologize to you for the way I acted this summer. I know now that God does not want me to be angry and selfish. I was acting terrible. God tells us to love our neighbors. You are my best friend, and I am sorry I hurt you. Last Saturday made me know that I should not put my future in danger."

"Why would your future be in danger if you stayed here?" asked Eliza curiously.

"Maybe you not know. Jed told me he could not marry me last Saturday," Katrina told her.

"I'm sorry, Katrina," Eliza said as she took Katrina's hand. "Will you be going back to Russia, then?"

"Yes, it is the best thing to do. I know now," Katrina said. "I know I can trust God to take care of me, and He knows my future. I can trust in God to have the best plan for my life."

"That is so true," Eliza said. "I'm glad you know that now. Will you still go to the Russian Orthodox Church in Siberia?"

"That is what I will do. There are no other churches but the Orthodox Church in Russia. We need people like your father to come to Russia to tell us about how we can be a personal friend with God. I will listen to the priest, but I want to get a Bible so I can learn more about God," Katrina said.

When they reached Erm's village, they scanned the crowd that worked feverishly to dry and salt fish for the winter. Others were pounding fat, berries, and nuts together and storing the mixture in seal bladders for the winter or for food when they traveled or when the men went hunting or fishing. Erm was nowhere in sight. They went to the Wolf House and asked for Erm.

"Not here," said her aunt. "She in the women's hut."

"Where is that?" Eliza asked.

"There," Erm's aunt said, pointing to a small hut at the back edge of the village.

Eliza and Katrina walked to the hut. A reed mat served as a door.

"Erm, are you in there?" Eliza asked.

"Yes, I am here," they heard Erm say.

"Can we come in?" Katrina asked.

"Yes, you can come in because you are women," Erm said.

Eliza pushed the mat aside and peered into the dark hut. Erm was sitting at the back edge of the hut. She was sitting on a pile of dried grasses and reeds. It appeared she did not have her leggings on, and she had covered her legs with a blanket.

"Why are you in here?" Katrina asked as she entered.

"I am woman now. I have the blood flow," Erm said. "I am unclean as long as I have blood flow. Women sent here when we have unclean time. Almost over. Maybe tomorrow."

"What happens when you become a woman?" Eliza asked.

"My aunt train me to do all the things women must do," Erm said. "I show I can be strong Tlingit woman."

"How do you show that you are a strong woman?" Katrina asked.

"Next week, I do many tasks. Show the women the baskets and cloth from reeds I make," Erm said. "Women will look at what I do. Decide if I good worker. Good workers help the clan to survive. If I not do well, I not be woman until I can pass their tests."

"If you don't pass the tests, what will happen then?" asked Eliza.

"I not marry Monutat this year. I need to wait until I can do things a strong Tlingit woman can do," Erm told them.

"Do you think you can do them?" Katrina asked.

"My aunt teach me these things from when I was a very little girl. She strong Tlingit woman and teach me very well. I think I do all the tasks they ask me to do. I make many baskets and bentwood boxes. I make parkas and dresses I wear. I sew the beads and make other decorations too," Erm said with confidence. "I just need to pass the women looking close to my work."

"I am sure you will pass. Your parka and dresses are beautiful. I didn't know you had made them," Eliza said.

"The one thing I not sure I can do is make an animal skin into a blanket. I have helped my aunt and my mother, but now I have to do it by myself," Erm said.

"What do you have to do to make a skin into a blanket?" Eliza asked.

"I eat … no, I …" Erm said as she moved her jaw up and down as if she were eating.

"Chew?" asked Eliza.

"Yes, I chew the skin. The water in my mouth helps the skin keep and be soft," Erm said.

"That sounds awful. Does it taste bad?" Katrina asked.

"Yes, but I use to it. It might not taste good to you," Erm told her. "My father out hunting for a skin now. I will chew and dry skin and chew and dry again all week long. I need to make seal bladders into bags to keep food in. I have many things to do."

"I cannot do any of those things," Katrina said. "I know how to wash clothes, cook, clean house, and do some sewing. I still need to practice that. I watch Meti make parka for our family, but I have only helped."

"Are you ready to get married so soon? You are very young to be married," Eliza said.

"If I pass woman test, I will be happy to marry Monutat," Erm said. "My aunt arrange it with Monutat's aunt. It is best to marry outside your clan. Monutat will live here now. A married couple will live at the women's village. I am already an aunt, and I must pass test so I can teach my brother's little girl."

"Why the mothers not teach the children? Our mothers teach us, and I do not have an aunt here to teach me," Katrina said.

"It is the way of my people. In the Wolf House, we are all one family. All parents take care of all children. The job of teaching is given to the aunt," Erm said. "It is just the way of the Tlingit."

"If you pass the test this week, when will Monutat and you get married?" asked Eliza.

"We have been preparing for our wedding potlatch since this summer. We still have many things to do. The things I do this week will be for the potlatch. I think we could be ready by end of the ninth moon," Erm said.

"That soon?" Katrina cried out.

"Yes. We need to do it before the winter comes. Wedding potlatches are in the fall," Erm said. "We have all spring and summer to prepare things."

"Can we come to your wedding potlatch?" asked Eliza.

"Yes. I want your whole families to come. I will let you know if I pass test and when to come for potlatch," Erm told them.

"I can't wait to see it!" Eliza exclaimed.

Chapter 25

When Eliza returned to her tent, she found her mother in bed sleeping next to Amos. Eliza tiptoed into the tent and looked closely at her mother. She never slept during the day. There was something different looking about Mother. She looked so small, so childlike. There were deep dark circles under her eyes. The sound of her struggling breath rasped through the tent.

Suddenly, Amos started his deep whooping-like cough and drooled phlegm from his mouth. Eliza was relieved to see that there was no blood in it. If there were blood in it, it would mean he was bleeding in his lungs. The blood was too much to pass into the bloodstream and would collect in the little sacs in his lungs. If there were blood in the lungs, he would eventually drown in his own blood. So far there had only been traces of it early in Amos's illness—and none since he had been given the shaman's tea.

Amos's cough awakened Mother. She rolled over so she could see Amos. Then she lay back down and began coughing from the effort.

"Mother, are you all right?" Eliza asked, leaning over the bed as far as she could.

"I am very sick," she mumbled. "Please go get your Father. He is at the alder tree, meeting with some of the men."

"I'll be right back," Eliza said as she raced out of the tent. She sprinted up the slope to where the church meeting was held. Dogs barked or followed her as she ran past. She pulled up her dress and petticoats to be able to run freely. Miners who saw her running jumped up to follow too.

Eliza reached the tree where her father sat with the shaman and several other Tlingit. She burst into the group, shouting, "Help, help! Father, Mother is deathly sick. Please come quickly!"

Father immediately jumped up, followed by the shaman. Eliza turned and followed them, as well as two of the Tlingit and the miners who had followed her up the hill.

When they arrived, the men could see that Mrs. Healy looked deathly pale. Eliza noticed that her skin seemed to hug her skull and hands. Blue veins were visible beneath her thinned skin.

"I'll go get the doctor!" one of the miners yelled as he raced off.

The shaman began speaking to the other two Tlingit in their native language, telling them to go to his house and bring certain herbs, roots, barks, and oils. The two raced off on silent moccasin feet.

The shaman looked Mother over closely and began quietly speaking Tlingit. He pulled an eagle feather from his hair and waved it over both Mother and Amos. He went to the fire pit and looked for a hot coal in the fire that had gone out long ago. He placed it on a small cupped rock and pulled herbs from his bag. They smoldered, and a wisp of smoke rose from the rock. The shaman waved the smoking herbs closely over Mother and Amos and continued a chant.

Eliza recognized the smell. It was peppermint, and she knew it was an excellent herb to clear sinus and airways. She thought that peppermint was the right choice to use to ease their coughs.

The Russian doctor, Dr. Strobel, rushed into the tent and pushed the shaman abruptly aside. "Why is this imposter here?" he roared. "Let me see the patients."

He felt Mother's and Amos's heads to determine whether they had fevers. Amos did not have a fever, but the doctor said that Mother had a slight fever. He listened to their hearts and lungs.

Turning to Father, Dr. Strobel said, "I believe she has caught the bacteria that developed in Amos's lungs from his accident. She looks very run-down and weak at this point. I will give you more of the medicine I gave you for Amos. You can see that it works, since Amos no longer has a fever."

Father took the bottle of medicine and shook hands with the doctor. After the doctor left, he called the shaman back into the tent. Father pulled Eliza into his arms. Father, the shaman, and Eliza prayed over the two sleeping specters that lay on the bed.

The two Tlingit came running into the tent, handing the shaman several bags and a sack of oil. They also brought two large stones that worked like a mortar and pestle. The shaman went outside and put various herbs, barks, and roots on the mortar. He began crushing them into a mixture that looked like the tea that he had given them for Amos. He placed it in a small leather bag and handed it to Father.

"Russian doctor think his medicine powerful, but I know that God has given us all the things we need right here to make people well," the shaman said. "I thank you, Brother Healy, for helping me to understand to what God I owe my thanks. I learn that your God is love and that He is the one that provides."

"Thank you, Thomas," Father said, shaking his hand.

"Thomas? Is that the shaman's name?" Eliza blurted out.

Laughing, the shaman said, "I accept Jesus into my heart, and I want a Christian name. I chose 'Thomas' because I have doubted so long that Jesus is Lord, just like Thomas in the Bible."

Eliza had learned long ago that the shaman did not need to be feared. She knew he came to the church meeting every Sunday and came to the Bible study her father held each Saturday afternoon.

"It is very nice to meet you, Thomas. Although you still know the shaman ways to heal, I thought there had been a change in you," Eliza said. "I don't think Dr. Strobel knows it is your medicine tea that is helping Amos. Now it will help my mother too."

Eliza's mother continued to be weak. Eliza stayed home and did all of the cooking, washing, and caring for Amos and her mother.

She faithfully administered both the Russian medicine and Thomas's medicine as she was instructed. Eliza fell into bed each night seeming as tired as her mother.

As Mother began to get better, she stopped taking the Russian medicine. She wasn't able to nurse Amos if she continued taking the medicine. Her milk was still Amos's main source of food, and it was important that he received nourishment. He hadn't liked the cow's milk that Father had purchased.

Eliza prepared rich broths and smooth soups for them to eat. She made them with fish, venison, or clams. She added potatoes and other root vegetables that Erm or Monutat brought her.

Each morning, her family prayed for her mother's and Amos's healing. Each day, Father and the Christian miners and Tlingit came to the alder tree to pray for them. Eliza knew there were others who prayed too. Katrina and Max went to the Orthodox church each day, lit candles, and prayed. Many prayers went up from the small town of Sitka for one of their most beloved ladies.

* * * *

August rolled into September. Each week, the temperature became colder. The fall rains seemed to never let up. Katrina and Eliza spent a lot of time together, often at Eliza's tent or strolling on the beach. Jed and Max often joined them on the weekends. Katrina and Max came regularly to church. Erm and Monutat came often. The six of them went for walks, or the girls would bring food for a picnic after church. Sunday was one day off her father had given her to enjoy. Being Sunday, Father would be in the tent after services, reading his Bible and taking care of her mother.

"I love these picnics," Jed would say as he lay back on a blanket. "Each of you girls brings great food. It is interesting how good the combinations of Tlingit, Russian, and American foods are."

Max said, "I sure do love American apple pie," as he shoveled another forkful into his mouth.

"I like Russian dumplings," Monutat added, rubbing his stomach.

"Nothing matches Erm's poached salmon with root vegetables," Jed said. "We eat well on these picnics."

They usually had their picnics on the slope where the church meetings were held. The large alder tree shaded them on sunny days and provided shelter if it rained. Eliza loved sitting with her back against the tree and looking out over the ocean and mountains. It was easy for the boys to lie back and close their eyes.

Eliza soon knew that Max snored. They would all laugh at him, and Katrina would punch him to roll over. Jed often sat with his back against the tree too. Their shoulders would touch, and she knew the warm feeling Erm had told Katrina and her about when Monutat touched her. It seemed to Eliza that Jed purposely bumped her arm or shoulder.

One day, Jed turned to her and asked, "How's school going these days? You haven't been asking me for so much help lately."

"Oh, Jed, I love teaching. I will miss it so much this winter. Now that the Tlingit are getting ready for winter, the girls don't come most of the time," Eliza said. "I have been helping with the older students more lately. I just hate the idea that I won't be able to teach anymore."

"Maybe you will," Jed said. "With the transfer in October, they will need teachers to teach the American and other children that are here in Sitka. You can become a licensed teacher when you are sixteen, and out here, you probably can continue to teach even though you will be only fifteen this year. The parents will just be glad there is a teacher at all."

"Do you really think so?" Eliza asked.

"Yes, I do," said Jed as he brushed her hand.

* * * *

As the Americans and Tlingit in Sitka got to know each other better, they became friendlier. The Tlingit realized that the Americans would look after their interests better. The Americans had started hunting for meat in the forests. Tlingit hunters often went with the hunters to teach them the ways of the woods. Eliza finally had the venison stew she so missed. She was always happy to see the American ships coming to the port, bringing more and more supplies.

Tlingit were allowed in the fort, and the Americans and Tlingit moved in and out of the fort freely. Eliza noticed that the Russians and Tlingit still avoided each other. The Russians were leaving soon, so it was not necessary to continue to harass the Tlingit. The Alaskan territory had belonged to America since April, but it had little jurisdiction over Alaska until after the governing power was transferred to the United States in October.

With the colder weather, the leaves on the alder trees had turned a brilliant yellow. Here and there on the mountain, other types of trees turned the various shades of reds and oranges, but most of the trees remained green. The pines, cedars, and other evergreens still dominated the forests.

Chapter 26

The late September day dawned cold and rainy. As Eliza peered from the tent flap, she pulled her sweater tighter across her chest. The gray sky made it seem like predawn. The sea looked as if it were boiling, and the waves were crashing against the shore.

"This doesn't seem like a very good day for a wedding," Eliza said.

Her father stirred up the fire and added more wood. The strong wind blew the smoke in and around the flaps of the tent. At least the front half of the tent was warm.

"No, it does not seem a good day for a wedding. We will have to wear our parkas if it stays this way," her father said.

"Oh, Edvard, will we ever get a house before winter?" Eliza's mother complained. "Now that Amos is well, I do not want him to get sick again from the cold."

"Our lottery number has not come up yet," her father said. "More of the Russians are leaving every day. As soon as our number comes up, we will choose a home. I hope it will be big enough to hold church in it for the winter."

Father brought the hot pots of corn mush and coffee into the tent. The family sat on their beds to eat breakfast and have devotions.

"This morning, I would like to talk about marriage. It is important to choose the right person," Father said. "I will read 1 Corinthians 6:14–16. 'Do not be bound to unbelievers. How can goodness be a partner with wickedness? How can light be a partner with darkness? What harmony can there be between Christ and the Devil? How can a believer be a partner with an unbeliever? And what union can there be between God's temple and idols? For we are the temple of the living God.'"

"Does that mean I shouldn't marry a man who doesn't believe in God?" asked Eliza.

"Yes. There should be three people in a marriage: a husband, a wife, and God. When God is not included or if only one person includes God and the other does not, many differences grow between the husband and wife," said Father. "It is very difficult when one is standing on God's promises and the other person is walking away from God."

"But some people who do not believe in God are very nice and do good things," said Eliza. "Mr. Guillard at the general store swears and drinks with the miners, but he is still very nice."

"Would you want to be married to a man like that?" asked Father.

"No!" Eliza exclaimed. "I would not want to hear those words he says or have him drink all of the time. I might become like that too."

"That is right," said Father. "You can see why that would be a difficult thing in a marriage. Loving someone means that you want to do all that you can for that person. Often, Christians are drawn away from God when they want to please their spouses who do not believe as they do."

"Erm and Monutat will live the Tlingit way, but she has asked me many questions about God, Jesus, and the Holy Spirit this summer," said Eliza. "What if she becomes a believer and Monutat doesn't?"

"Monutat and I have talked many times after church, and I think he is beginning to understand more about being a believer in Christ," said Father. "Perhaps in time they both will believe. We should pray that they will accept Christ as their Savior."

Eliza nodded. "I will continue to pray for them."

The rain stopped beating on the roof of the tent. Eliza peeked out the tent door. It was still cloudy, and mist hung in the air. The mountain peaks were hidden by a heavy fog that danced with the movement of the wind.

"Maybe it will clear up by this afternoon," Eliza said hopefully. "I don't see the sun, but maybe it will at least stop raining for Erm's wedding."

"We can hope and pray," said Mother.

They prayed that God would bless the day and Erm's marriage. They asked that God's Spirit would move in Erm's and Monutat's hearts and that they would feel God's leading.

Amos had fallen asleep. Mother wanted him to have a good nap, since they might be out late. While Amos slept, Father continued to read the Bible. Mother worked on mending one of Father's shirts, and Eliza wrote in her journal about the many changes in her life.

Mother and Amos were almost well. The church continued to grow, and more and more people were coming to Christ. God was definitely blessing their work.

She wrote about Jed and how her feelings for him were growing. She wrote a prayer in her journal, asking God to reveal His plan for her life and if Jed were a part of it.

After a quick lunch of leftover corn bread and stew, they prepared to go to Erm's village.

When they were ready to leave, they heard someone speaking in Russian outside their tent. When Eliza looked out, she saw Katrina and her family walking up the beach. Mr. Voronov was dressed in a full Russian military uniform of red wool. Mrs. Voronov wore a blue velvet dress with a fur cape over her shoulders and a matching fur hat.

"Katrina, can we walk together with you and your family?" Eliza asked.

"That is why we are coming this way," said Katrina. "We thought it would be fun to go all together."

"Good day to you," Father said as he shook hands with Mr. Voronov. "We are just ready to go, and we would be pleased to walk with you to the village."

Mother took Mrs. Voronov's arm, and they began walking through the tent city. As they passed Jed's tent, Father called out to Jed. Jed poked his head out.

"Are you ready to go to the wedding?" Father asked.

"Yes, sir," Jed said as he pulled a leather coat over his suit.

Eliza had never seen Jed in a suit before, and she thought he looked quite handsome. Jed fell into the line with Max, who had been very quiet. He was leaving soon, and he was very aware of Jed and Eliza's growing relationship. Was that what made him so quiet lately?

Although the rain had stopped, the path was muddy, and wisps of fog floated among the trees. The air was crisp as they walked through the fallen leaves of the alder trees.

"I still cannot believe Erm is getting married today. Although she had to wait a month, she still seems too young to be married," Eliza said. "I won't even think about getting married until I am eighteen."

"I'm eighteen, and I cannot even think of getting married at this age," said Jed. "I have so many things I want to do before I settle down to get married. I couldn't go traipsing off to search for gold and adventure and drag a wife all over the territory."

"My father said I had to wait to get married too. I am not old enough, and it will take time to find the proper man for me to marry," Katrina said. "I am glad I do not need to get married so soon. I still have much to learn about running a household."

"How about you, Eliza? When will your father think that you will be ready to get married?" Max asked.

"As I said before, not soon, so don't get any ideas about staying here for my sake," Eliza said.

CHAPTER 27

They all were laughing as they neared the Tlingit village, but they quieted as they heard the sounds of drums and singing. Everyone in the village was inside the Wolf House, so they entered quietly and stood to the side. Their entrance caused surprised stares from the two Tlingit clans. There had never been an American or Russian family at a wedding potlatch. There were so many people that the entire lodge was crowded. People sat on the upper as well as the lower benches used for beds.

In the center of the lodge, the fire pit was full of blazing wood. Smoke filled the air as it slowly rose to the smoke hole in the roof. Dancers were dancing around the fire to the beat of the drums. Each dance had a different rhythm in step with the drums. In the third dance, Monutat joined the dancers.

He was dressed in a marten-skin robe with beautiful beading and a fur trim at the bottom of the shirt. He wore matching pants with matching colors and designs. His mukluks were also white and trimmed with soft white fur. The other dancers dressed in the yellow robes of the Raven Clan soon moved away, and only Monutat was left to dance. He stooped down with his hands to his sides. Then he rose and moved his arms as if he were flying and soaring around the fire. On occasion, he kneeled down and pretended to grab something from the floor, and then off he would soar again.

Eliza was spellbound. She could not imagine that a man could be so graceful. As she watched, she realized that he was pretending to be a raven, representing his clan. As she looked around the room, she saw men wearing yellow robes with similarly intricate black-and-white figures representing animals. They were similar to the Eagle Clan's red robes.

When the dance was over, Eliza looked around for Erm, but she could not see her anywhere. Then the singing began, and men in the red robes danced several dances. Finally, a group of women brought a blanket from a back corner of the room and placed it in the spot opposite the door, a place of honor. Everyone watched as Erm came from that back corner and danced down the pathway the women had made. She too lifted her arms, soaring as she moved. Her moves were lighter and more graceful as she moved to the fire and continued to dance.

Eliza realized with the continued soaring up and down and a slight flap of her arms from time to time that Erm was imitating the moves of an eagle, representing her clan. She moved her feet in a steady rhythm as she spun and swooped. The drums beat fast and slow rhythms, and Erm matched their beat.

Soon, Monutat joined her, and they wove in and out and around each other. Monutat continued with his raven dance and Erm with her eagle dance. Then the drumbeat changed, and they danced with arms touching and moved in perfect unison.

Erm's face was aglow with happiness. She was also dressed in a beautifully embroidered and beaded marten robe. Underneath the robe, she wore a white beaded dress and leggings. Eliza thought they both looked so beautiful. Throughout the dance, Erm kept her head bowed and did not look at Monutat. At the end of the dance, she looked directly into Monutat's face and into his eyes. They danced slowly in rhythm with one another.

Finally, they both went to sit on the blanket that had been placed on the floor. The crowd parted, and Eliza could see a table made of cedar planks on six legs. It was filled with all types of bowls and baskets of food. As they lifted the covers, wonderful and strange smells filled the air.

Everyone crowded in to fill wooden bowls with food from the table. Eliza and the others moved along with the crowd. Eliza and Katrina picked up bowls and began moving down the table. Women and girls continually refilled the large baskets of corn bread, venison roast, turkey, salmon, stews, and other things that Eliza couldn't identify. As she neared the end of the table, a strong smell arose. It smelled like rotting fish. When she reached the bowl, she peered in. Fish heads floated in salty brine.

"What is this?" Eliza whispered to Katrina.

"These are the stink heads that Erm was making last spring. Remember when she told us they buried fish heads in the ground with seaweed and seawater? This is what it make," Katrina said.

"Are you going to eat it?" Eliza asked.

"No, but you should try a little bit. It is Erm's favorite dish, and these are probably the ones she made," Katrina said. "I wonder if she knew she might be using it for her wedding."

The Tlingit were sitting all around on the floor or on the sleeping benches around the room. When the Healys and the Voronovs had filled their plates, several men brought benches for them to sit on.

Eliza looked at her bowl. She wasn't sure she could eat anything until the smell of the fish heads was gone. It made her whole bowl of food smell like rotten fish. Gingerly, she picked up the small piece she had taken. As she examined it, she could see the jawbone and eyes of the dead salmon head. As she looked around, she saw that the Tlingit were chewing and sucking on the bones to remove the meat. Eliza sucked a tiny piece of the meat into her mouth. Her eyes flew open, and she covered her mouth with her hand. She didn't know what else to do but swallow it down.

Katrina laughed with her hand over her mouth. "Good, no?" she said.

Eliza's eyes were tearing, and her stomach protested. "I think I might be sick," she said.

"Eat some corn bread. It will help to get the taste from your mouth," Katrina advised, giggling again.

"That was awful! Why didn't you warn me?" Eliza asked.

"I did. I said I wasn't taking any." Katrina laughed.

Eliza picked at her other food, but the smell of the stink heads still lingered. She looked at the Tlingit who seemed to be enjoying it very much. She noticed that her and Katrina's parents were picking at their food too, while Max and Jed looked like they ate this type of food every day.

Erm and Monutat rose from the blanket and, with Erm's family, went to the other end of the lodge. They returned with piles of gifts. They were not gifts for the bride and bridegroom, but they began handing out the gifts to the people around the room. As one's arms were emptied, the gift bearer retreated into the darkness and brought more. They gave out fur blankets, bentwood boxes, wool blankets from the Russian-American Company's general store, baskets, spoons, and bowls. The men received carved spears, knives, snowshoes, harpoons, fishing nets, and other equipment they might need for hunting and fishing.

When they came to the Healys, Erm gave each of them a fur blanket.

"You will need them this winter," Erm said.

Amos received a carved wolf to play with.

To the Voronovs, they gave smaller items—beaded necklaces for Katrina and her mother, a knife with a handle made from deer antlers, and a small carved totem pole.

"These things are for you to remember us here in Alaska," Monutat said.

"These things will fit easily in your trunks," Erm said.

Monutat turned to Jed. "We have a special gift for you, Jed," he said as he disappeared outside. When he came back, he brought one of Saqua's husky puppies. "A miner needs a dog to keep him company, to catch rabbits, and to guard his claim. She will make a start for a dogsled team."

The six-month-old puppy looked at them all with her white eyes with the black rings around them. It was a beautiful, strong puppy with black, gray, and white fur. Jed thanked Monutat and Erm for his gift.

"We have gifts for you too," Eliza said as she brought out a dress-length of cloth wrapped in brown paper.

The Voronovs gave her a Russian cloth that Katrina had woven for them.

"No, we cannot accept them," Erm said. "Our way is to give gifts to the people who come and honor us with their presence at our marriage. My family, Monutat, and I have been working on these gifts since July."

Mother and Mrs. Voronov thanked Monutat and Erm for their gifts. Amos had fallen asleep, and there was a long walk home. Eliza and Katrina gave Erm a hug as they left.

The Healys and the Voronovs walked away from the lodge to the sounds of drums, singing, and shouts. The potlatch would last for two more days.

On the walk home, Eliza asked, "Father, when did they get married? There was no pastor or priest and not even the shaman to marry them."

"Remember the last dance where Erm came out of the corner and then Monutat joined her? At the end of the dance, they danced together. It is a symbol of the two clans joining and Monutat and Erm becoming one and being considered married," Father said.

The eight people, along with Amos, trudged home in the crisp fall night, lost in their own thoughts about the day.

CHAPTER 28

The whole town of Sitka was excited by the upcoming celebration of the transfer of the Alaska Territory from tsarist Russian ownership to American ownership. More Americans came to Sitka on every ship that sailed into the port, bringing the many supplies the town needed. American soldiers were coming for the celebration. They were often seen walking around town. Russian citizens began sailing to Siberia for the long trips to their various homes.

The ceremony for the exchange was to be held on Castle Hill. The hill was formed from a hard rock that the glaciers couldn't push into the sea. On the small hill, a large two-story house stood. On the top was a lighthouse with four seal-oil lamps that guided the ships into port. It was called Baranof Castle, named after the past Russian governor. Now Prince Maksutov lived there. The large house was surrounded by several cannons and a flagpole flying the Russian flag.

Eliza and her friends could hardly wait until the exciting day would come. They talked often of their plans for the future. Eliza's greatest hope was that her family would get a house as the weather continued to get colder and colder. Erm and Monutat were working hard to lay in supplies for the long, dark winter. They were glad that Monutat was a good hunter, since the village supply of dried salmon wasn't as plentiful this year. Katrina and Max talked sadly of returning to Russia. For them, Alaska had been their home for ten years. They hardly remembered what their Russian village looked like anymore.

Max had become very serious as the time for them to leave drew nearer. Eliza liked the old joking Max better. Now he seemed so sad. She knew from his actions and words that he cared for her, but she knew it would be better for him to return to Russia. He would meet a Russian girl, and that would be better for him, Eliza thought.

"What has your family decided to do, Katrina?" asked Eliza one day.

"After the ceremony, we will all be going back to Russia. Father needs to be here to take part in the Russian military parade. Only one hundred of the soldiers were asked to stay," Katrina told her.

"Are you going too, Max, or are you going to stay to go trapping?" Eliza wanted to know.

"My father said I need to go back with the family. I must carry on the family tradition and serve in the Russian army. There is good trapping in Russia too," Max said. "I will trap there until I am old enough to come back to Alaska on my own."

"What about you and Monutat?" Katrina asked Erm. "Will you continue to live in the Wolf House at your village?"

"Yes. I become a member of my wife's family. We will have a space in her lodge," Monutat said. "I will hunt with the Eagle Clan now."

"Monutat is a good hunter and fisherman," Erm said proudly. "He has already been honored for his skills."

Just then, Jed arrived with his new puppy.

"Hi, Jed," Eliza said. "Have you decided on a name for your dog yet?"

"Yes, I am calling her Monty. She is named after Monutat, since she is such a valued gift," Jed said as he tousled Monty's fur. The dog looked adoringly at Jed.

"We have been talking about what we will do after the ceremony," Eliza said. "What will you do? Are you in the lottery for a place to live?"

"I'm not sure what I will do," Jed said. "There are a lot of reasons to stay here, but my stake is not rich in gold. I hear that there is gold just lying on the beach across from Juneau. All you need to do is pick it up. I'm thinking about going up there to try my luck."

Eliza was disappointed at this news. She thought she would be able to continue her friendship with Jed. If he went to Juneau, she would probably never see him again.

"Would you ever come back?" Eliza asked.

"Yes, I will come back," Jed said with a sly smile on his face.

CHAPTER 29

October 18, 1867 dawned brisk and cold. Everyone from the Sitka area and beyond was down at the base of Castle Hill, waiting for the ceremony to start. As Eliza looked around the crowd, she could see that most of the Tlingit tribes in the area were there. Chinese, Norwegian, French, Russian, and American people were scattered throughout the crowd.

"When will the ceremony start?" asked Eliza.

"The American dignitaries and soldiers are not here yet," Jed replied.

"Why not? They must know they are to be here today," Eliza asked.

"Ships do not always keep on schedule. The seas are rough today, and they may be having trouble getting here," her father said.

The crowd began to get restless as the day wore on. Many of the men went off to the saloon to wait for the ceremony. Women packed up their children and took them home for lunch. Eliza and her friends went to sit on the steps of Saint Michael's Cathedral to eat the lunches the girls had packed. From this vantage point, they could see Castle Hill and the waterfront to be able to see the ship as it came in.

At about three o'clock in the afternoon, the boom of a cannon split the air. As the friends looked down the street, they could see a large ship sail into port. It had the name USS *Ossipee* painted on the bow. The decks were filled with American soldiers and men in top hats like the one Abraham Lincoln wore. An American flag flew over the ship. The soldiers and men disembarked and lined up on the shore. There seemed to be three times as many American soldiers as Russian. The Russian soldiers had been standing at the ready all day.

Military bands began to play. With great pomp, the soldiers marched up Castle Hill. The Russian soldiers stood on the left side of the flagpole. The Russian flag was still flying. The Americans marched to the right side of the flagpole.

"I heard there might be some demonstrations against this transfer," Jed told them as they watched.

"The Russian soldiers are upset that Alaska transferred to America," Max said. "It's hard for Russia to send supplies, but we think it good for Russia to keep Alaska. The Alaska Russians know many resources Russia can use."

"I hope not. This should be a solemn occasion," Eliza said.

Katrina and Max were quiet.

Erm said, "It will be different now that the Americans are here. I have heard the elders from our village say they fear what the Americans will do. We hear the Indians down south are not treated well."

When all of the soldiers were in formation, the *Ossipee* fired its cannons in a salute to the Russian flag, and the Russian batteries on the hill answered back.

As the Russian flag was lowered, it got caught on the flagpole. A young Russian soldier tried to continue to pull it on down, but it wouldn't budge. He tried many times. Finally, other soldiers hefted him up on their shoulders so that he could reach where the flag was stuck. Then the men continued the lowering of the Russian flag.

"I think the Russians do not want to leave Alaska," Max said. "Even the flag does not want to leave."

The American flag was properly attached to the flagpole. As it began its ascent by General Rousseau, the Russian battery fired a cannon salute to the American flag, and the *Ossipee*'s cannons answered back. The flag reached the top as the last American cannon was fired and echoed on the mountains around Sitka.

The Russian General Pestchouroff stepped up to General Rousseau and said, "General Rousseau, by the authority from His Majesty the Emperor of Russia, I transfer to the United States the Territory of Alaska."

With those few words, Alaska became part of the United States. The crowd roared as the ceremony ended. Eliza was excited by the transfer, but as she looked at Katrina and Max, she knew they were not feeling the same joy. Quickly and silently, she sent a prayer up to God to keep them safe and bring them belief in Jesus and happiness.

"When will you leave?" Eliza asked Katrina.

"We leave tomorrow with the Russian soldiers," Katrina said. "Do you have a house yet?"

"No, but we are supposed to get our lottery number tomorrow, since so many Russian families are leaving. I can't wait to get out of that tent," Eliza said. "Tomorrow night, we hope to be in a house."

"I am going to miss all of you when we leave," Katrina said with tears in her eyes. "I didn't know we would have to leave so soon. Father is to report to his new post in two months. We need to leave now if we are going to get to Russia in time."

"I will miss you too," Eliza said as she hugged her. "When does your ship leave?"

"We are to load up our things by noon," Katrina said.

"We will all come and help you and then see you off," Jed said, shaking hands with Max.

"Come to our house about eleven o'clock. We will be taking our things down to the wharf then to be loaded," Katrina said.

Eliza and Erm watched Katrina and Max as they walked up Barrack Road to their house to pack up the things they would be taking back to Russia with them.

"What will I do without Katrina? She has been a good friend," Eliza said. "And even though Max can be a pain in the head, I will miss him too. He is a good friend too."

"I am still here," said Erm.

"Oh, I know," Eliza said as she threw her arms around Erm. "You will always be my friend, but now that you are married, you will be too busy to visit. And during the winter, it will be too cold to walk to the village in the snow."

"We will be coming into Sitka from time to time for supplies," said Erm.

"How will you get here through the snow?" Eliza asked.

"Listen for the dogs barking when we come with our dogsled." Erm smiled. "We will be back in spring after the spring eulachon fish camp. You will not be alone."

"Hey, don't forget about me! I'll be here!" Jed said.

Chapter 30

Eliza walked with her father to the land office early the next morning. When they arrived, a line snaked down the boardwalk outside the office.

"What number are they on?" Father asked the man ahead of them.

"They're on 130," the man said. "I'm 150."

"We have 149," Eliza said.

"You're in front of me," the man said as he stepped back.

"Why, thank you," her father said to the man.

"Do you think we will get into the office by eleven o'clock?" Eliza asked her father. "That's when Katrina said to come to say good-bye."

"I don't know how long they take with each person," Father said.

The man behind them said, "They go pretty slow. I have been waiting since six o'clock this morning, and now it is ten o'clock. When we check in, someone will take us to look at two houses. We may choose the one we want. Do you have just one child?"

"No. I have a son at the tent with my wife," Father said.

"You have a chance to look at some of the bigger houses, then. The smaller ones are given to the single men or families with no children," the man said.

"Oh, Father, won't it be grand if we could have one of the bigger houses?" exclaimed Eliza.

"I have been praying that God would give us a house large enough to hold the church in during the winter months," her father said. "But we will be content with what God provides for us."

Just then, the door of the office opened, and a man and woman came out with an agent to go look at the two houses they drew. They moved up one place. Now there were ten people in front of them. By ten thirty, they were still five spaces from the door. The line was moving slowly.

"I promised Katrina and Max that I would help get their things down to the ship. Can I go to Katrina's house now?" Eliza asked her father.

"You might as well go. It looks like I may be standing in this line for another hour or more," Father said as he glanced back of them. "The poor people at the end of this line, I hope they will get a house. But check with your mother to see if she needs any help. I think she was going to start packing up the tent in case we do get a house today."

"Okay!" Eliza yelled over her shoulder as she raced to the tent. She whipped through the tent flap and almost ran into Mother with her arms full of dishes.

"Do you need any help?" Eliza asked breathlessly. "I'm supposed to go to help Katrina and Max get their things down to the ship for Russia. They said come before eleven o'clock."

Mother pulled her pocket watch from her apron pocket. "If you could pack your things, it would be a help."

Eliza took the things sitting on her trunk and threw them into a corner of the trunk. She grabbed her other two dresses from the hook above her bed, rolled them up, and threw those in too. She had to sit on the trunk lid to get it closed.

"Eliza!" Mother said. "Take those things out and fold them properly. Remember we will need to get your quilt in there too."

Eliza quickly removed the items and folded them carefully. "Okay, there will be room for my quilt and linens. Can I go now?"

"You might as well." Mother laughed. "Tell the Voronovs good-bye for me."

Eliza ran back to Lincoln Street and started up Barracks Street. She walked up two streets, and on the corner of Barracks and Princess Streets, she saw the Voronovs loading a cart with their trunks and boxes. Jed, Monutat, and Erm were already there. Eliza helped bring out the last of the boxes.

The men tied up the load and began pulling the cart down the hill on Barracks Street. Jed and Monutat were guiding the cart in the front, while Max and Mr. Voronov steadied the cart. All of the women were carrying large baskets of food for the long voyage home.

"We will at least have a small cabin on the ship, but they do not provide food for us," Katrina said. "I am glad we have a room this time. When we came ten years ago, we could either stay on deck or go down to the hold and sleep. It stank so much down there with so many people. We came in the summer, so we could sleep on the deck most nights."

"It will be a bit cold to stay on deck now," Eliza said. "It will be good to have a small room, at least."

When they reached the bottom of the hill, Jed and Monutat turned right and pulled the cart to the docks with Max and his father pushing.

"I am glad you came to help," Max said to Jed and Monutat. "I don't think Father and I could have handled it alone."

A sailor came through the crowd calling the names of the next family to board the ship. "Voronov! Voronov!" he called.

"Here we are!" Mr. Voronov shouted. Turning to the group around the cart, he said, "Come. We must get loaded up."

Monutat, Jed, and Max took the trunks and boxes up the gangplank, while the women guarded the remaining items on the cart.

"Oh, Eliza and Erm, this is so hard," Katrina said as she turned to hug her friends. "I do not even remember my home in Siberia or my family there. It will seem like I am going to another new place. I am leaving the best friends I have ever had."

"Katrina, I'll miss you so much." Eliza cried into Katrina's shoulder. They hugged for a long time.

"Erm, you have been my friend for a long time. I will miss you too," Katrina said. "You will be so busy being Monutat's wife that you will not have time to think of me."

"Yes, I will," Erm said. "I love Monutat, but I love you too. I think Eliza and I will talk about what a good friend you have been forever."

All three girls hugged each other.

The last of the boxes and trunks had been taken into the ship. Mr. Voronov and Max came down to tell everyone good-bye.

"Eliza," Max said as he tapped her on the shoulder and pushed a fur collar around her neck. "Will you wait for me to come back?"

"I would be an old maid if I had to wait that long," Eliza said. "Is this fur for me?"

"Yes," Max said. "I made it just for you to keep your neck warm and to remember me."

"Thank you for the gift," Eliza said as she stroked the smooth fur.

Max took her hand and bowed and kissed it. "I will be back someday." Then he turned abruptly and strolled to the ship.

Eliza and Erm picked up the baskets they had carried down to the ship and handed them to Katrina and Mrs. Voronov. They watched Katrina and her family board the ship. When they got to the rail, they all waved good-bye to the four who remained on shore.

Eliza waved and waved. Even Erm raised her arm to wave. Jed and Monutat had told Max good-bye on the ship when they had made their last trip on board. Jed gave big waves with both arms.

The Voronovs left the rail to prepare for the ship to sail. All of the women needed to clear the decks so that the men could get the ship under way. Eliza stood watching the ship, hoping Katrina would appear again, but she didn't.

"Come. Let's go," Jed said gently.

Tears ran down Eliza's face, and she held Erm around the shoulders.

"We must go," Monutat said. "I must join the men for a hunt tonight. I must go to the village to get ready."

Jed and Eliza remained a few more minutes to watch the ship.

"Do you think your father has found a house?" Jed said as he led her toward her tent.

"Oh, I forgot all about that," Eliza said. "I don't know. He must by now."

They walked slowly toward the tent. Jed stopped Eliza as they reached Lincoln Street. "I have something very important to ask you. Would you mind if I asked your father whether I could court you?"

Eliza gasped. "Why would you want to court me?"

"I know you are young, but I want to let you and your father know my intentions. I like you very much and enjoy your spirit and sense of adventure. I will never forget the day you went down in my mine," Jed said. "You are just the kind of girl who would keep my life interesting."

Eliza dropped her chin in thought. "I don't know whether Father will agree, but yes, you may ask him," said Eliza with rosy cheeks and a smile.

CHAPTER 31

W hen they reached Eliza's tent, her mother and father were quickly packing their things into the trunks.

"We have a house!" Mother exclaimed. "We are moving there today. We will sleep in a house tonight!"

"Where?" Eliza asked as she folded her quilt and put it in her trunk with her other things.

"It's up near the Russian cemetery," Father said. "As soon as we get our things ready, we will head up there. Jed, would you mind helping us today?"

"No problem," Jed said as he hoisted a bed frame on his shoulder.

Eliza and her mother continued to get their things together while Amos ran around, confused by all of the activity.

When the men came back, they were pulling the cart the Voronovs had used to carry their things to the ship. They loaded it with the rest of their belongings, including the fur blankets that Erm and Monutat had given them.

Father and Jed pulled the cart up Lincoln Street and then turned up Barracks Street. Both of them had big smiles on their faces.

"It is great that we have a house, but why are you two grinning so much?" Eliza asked.

"You will see," Father said as they stopped at the corner of Barracks and Princess Streets.

"This is Katrina's house!" Eliza cried. "Are we going to live in Katrina's house?"

"Yes. It will be big enough to hold church in, and it is a suitable house for Jed to court you," Father said.

Jed and Eliza looked at each other with smiles on their faces.

They walked into the front door. They entered the large room that served as a sitting room to the left of the door. It had a fireplace, and a piano sat at the end of the room.

To the right of the door was a large archway with beautiful woodwork to enter a room that served as the dining room.

"I think these two rooms will hold the benches from the clearing and will be big enough for our church. We can store the benches against the dining room's back wall. The kitchen has a small table for the four of us," Father said.

"And a piano!" Mother exclaimed. She hurried to the piano, gently running her fingers over the keys.

Father led the family to the room behind the dining room. Cupboards were built into the left corner with a sink and pump. At the far end of the kitchen stood a cast-iron stove. On the right side sat a small table with four stools.

Mother cried out when she saw her new kitchen. She turned and hugged her husband. "Oh, thank you, Edvard!" she cried. "It is a perfect house. It even has the piano I prayed for. I don't understand why the Voronovs left their piano, though."

"Over ten years, you can collect a lot of things. They ordered the piano the third year they were here, but they were not allowed to take it with them back to Russia," Father said. "When I visited their house during the lottery, I told them we would take their house. Once they knew we had their house, they decided to leave it. They know you love to play the piano and that we would need one for our church, so they gave it to us with their blessings. We continue to see how generous the Voronovs are.

"Across the hall is a bedroom for us and Amos until he gets older and can move into one of the bedrooms upstairs. Eliza can choose the one she wants, and then Amos will have the other one," Father said.

Eliza ran up the stairs next to the downstairs bedroom. She peeked into each of the bedrooms. One faced the Russian cemetery, and the other one faced the sea. She walked into the room facing the sea. She knew this must have been Katrina's room by the painted flowers on the door and window frames. She looked out the window and saw the lay of the town, the mountains on Japonski Island, and the ravens that were constantly cawing and flying around the town.

When she came downstairs, the men were carrying their boxes and trunks into the house. Mother was singing merrily in the kitchen as she built a fire in the stove. Behind the kitchen was a room that served as a woodshed and latrine. They would not even need to go outside to get wood and use the facilities. The long porch on the back still held Mrs. Voronov's washtubs and line.

"To which room should we take your bed and mattress?" Father asked as he brought them in. Jed was behind him with her mattress.

"The one on the right, which faces the sea," she told them. "I am sure it was Katrina's room. It will remind me of her."

Eliza went into the sitting room and started a fire in the fireplace. Then she stood up and looked around the room for a moment.

When her father came back downstairs, Eliza asked, "Father, do you think I could have a school here during the week for the American children that are coming? I love to teach so much."

"That might be a good idea. We will have to talk about that," her father replied as he brought in the last blanket.

"May I have a word with you, Eliza?" Jed asked. "Please sit down here on the piano bench. I want to tell you my plans too. I found a room at the hotel and will be staying there this winter. But in the spring, I am going to Juneau to pan for the gold they are finding right on the beach. I plan to go for two years. By then, I hope to have enough money to come back. You will almost be seventeen, and I will be twenty. It will be a more appropriate time for us to court, your father said."

Eliza stared at Jed. "You mean you will be deserting me too?"

"I will be here for six more months, and we can see each other this winter. But in the summer, I must go to find the money I will need to support us. By that time of year, you can get to Erm's village to visit her. Even though she is married, you can still be friends."

"I guess you are right, but I will miss you. Do you have to go for two years?" Eliza asked.

"Do you think you will forget me by then?" Jed laughed.

"No, I won't forget you. It's just that it seems like such a long time."

"They have a steamboat that travels between Juneau and Sitka. I can come visit you from time to time," Jed told her. "And I will spend most of the winter here."

Just then, they heard a dog barking outside the door. "I guess Monty has tracked me down," Jed said. "I'd better get going and get my things to the hotel."

Eliza's father came back into the sitting room after helping her mother put things away. "Even Amos will have his own bed. We will make a mattress that fits into the alcove behind the fireplace. He will stay nice and warm there. Jed, is that your dog barking?"

"Yes, I'm afraid it is, sir. I need to get back to my tent to pack up my few things and mining equipment and move to the hotel. I plan to be warmer tonight too."

"Thanks so much for your help today," Father said. "I assume we will be seeing you around here."

"Yes, sir. Will you need help moving the church benches up here?" Jed asked.

"Yes. That would be great. I will ask a few of the miners to help too," Father replied. "How about coming by in two days? That will give us time to settle and have the benches ready for this Sunday."

"All right, I'll see you in a couple of days," Jed said as he stepped outside.

Eliza looked out the window and watched Jed tousle the fur on Monty's head. Monty responded by putting her feet up on Jed's chest. She heard Jed say, "Down, girl." Monty immediately got down, wagging her tail until her whole body was moving back and forth. Eliza watched as they turned the corner and headed down Barracks Street.

The Healys ate the best dinner they had had since they had arrived in Alaska. Eliza's mother was elated to finally have a stove to cook on and a real oven in which to bake bread.

After dinner, Eliza went up to her room to put her things away and make her bed. She lit a candle before she went up the stairs. It glowed in the darkness of the Alaskan early night.

After making her bed, she put her nightgown on near the grate that allowed heat to rise into her room. Wrapped in her grandmother's quilt, she sat on the end of her bed. She could see out her window, and she watched the moon sparkle over the water in Sitka Bay.

"Dear Father in heaven. Thank You for this house You have provided for us. Thank You for Jed and for his plans for us. Give me the wisdom to know if he is the right person for me to marry. I know I'm not perfect; only You and Christ can help me be worthy of Your favor. If it is Your desire for me to start a school and teach children, then let Your plan for me be done. If it is not Your will, please provide me with useful work for You. Thank You, Father. In Jesus's precious name, amen."

Eliza crawled into her bed with her grandmother's quilt and Erm's fur blanket covering her in Katrina's room.

"I am surrounded by my friends," Eliza whispered as she fell asleep.